Bounty Hunter

Lynette Eason

HARLEQUIN® LOVE INSPIRED® SUSPENSE

Special thanks and acknowledgment to Lynette Eason for her participation in the Classified K-9 Unit miniseries.

LOVE INSPIRED BOOKS

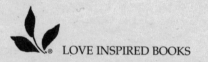

ISBN-13: 978-0-373-67833-4

Bounty Hunter

This edition published by arrangement with Love Inspired Books.

www.Harlequin.com

Printed in U.S.A.

Do not take revenge, my dear friends, but leave room for God's wrath, for it is written: "It is mine to avenge; I will repay," says the Lord.

–*Romans* 12:19

Dedicated to all of the K-9 officers, two-legged and four, who put their lives on the line on a daily basis.

ONE

A simple twitch of his finger and his sister's killer would be gone. His two-month quest to find Van Blackman would be over. Riley Martelli took one more long look at the man in his sights then lowered the weapon.

But he could never kill someone in cold blood. Not even the man who'd murdered his sister and put his six-year-old nephew, Asher, in the hospital with a bullet lodged near his spine.

Being a bounty hunter could be a dangerous line of work. Sometimes more dangerous than his days of being a beat cop.

It definitely had its ups and downs. Bringing in fugitives topped his list of things that made life worth living. But the stakes had never been higher. He just had to figure out how to capture Blackman without getting killed.

In the last year since changing professions, he'd been through some tough times and barely escaped with his life.

And yet none of that had dampened his determination to bring those fleeing the law to justice.

Especially this one. This one was personal.

Which was why he now found himself outside the small town of Drum Creek, Colorado, just as the sun was getting ready to go down. With little daylight left, Riley needed to quickly figure out how to approach the man and safely bring him in.

Van knelt, but Riley couldn't see what he was doing. Soon, small puffs of smoke drifted from the patch of ground. Was he building a fire? Did that mean he was planning to stay for a while?

Riley settled the gun back on his shoulder and got a better look with the scope. Van crouched over the small flame, pushing the contents as though trying to encourage a larger blaze. Riley lowered the weapon.

Now, in a very secluded area of Colorado's Rocky Mountain National Park, Van moved to stand next to a black SUV just a few yards ahead of him. Grand Lake was calm and serene behind him. A sense of peace and satisfaction flooded Riley even as his adrenaline spiked. It might be July in Colorado, but it was cold at night, dropping into the forties. Van wore a black ski cap pulled low over his ears, but his tall height and broad shoulders were harder to disguise. Riley's heart pounded. Finally, he was going to make his sister's killer pay. He shifted the rifle on his shoulder for one more look through the scope. He scanned his prey's body, watched the way he held his hands. His target kept touching his hip, which meant he probably had a gun there.

The man turned and Riley now had a full-on view of his face—and his heart stuttered.

It wasn't Van Blackman.

Disappointment shot through him. He had the wrong man. Riley lowered the rifle with a frustrated sigh. Then frowned and lifted it to stare through the scope once again. The man's face was familiar. Where had he seen him before? Television? Yeah, that was it. Could it be—? He focused again.

Yep. That was the missing FBI agent that had been all over the news lately. Morrow was his last name. Jack? Jeff? No, Jake. Jake Morrow. And there was a hundred thousand dollars being offered as a reward for his safe return.

It had been reported that he'd been kidnapped by the Dupree crime family and that he might have escaped, but still needed help.

The Dupree family had long been on the FBI's Most Wanted list, and from what Riley had been able to piece together, the feds had almost managed to capture them. Only things had gone wrong in a raid on a warehouse in Los Angeles.

While tracking Reginald Dupree and his uncle Angus Dupree, Morrow had disappeared from the warehouse. From what Riley remembered, a Dupree helicopter was able to get away during the shootout. It was suspected that Morrow was on that chopper, held against his will by Angus. Reginald and two of his associates had subsequently been arrested and were still in custody.

The weird thing was, Jake had been spotted all over the country, but the last report had him near Billings, Montana. So, of all places for him to show up, why here?

Riley lowered the rifle yet again and stood. “Special Agent Jake Morrow?”

The man froze and Riley raised his hands, along with the rifle, over his head and started walking slowly toward him. He stayed on the path that led to the little campsite clearing, bypassing the large rocks and tangled bushes as well as enormous trees. “I’m Riley Martelli. I’m a bounty hunter and I’ve been tracking a guy. I thought you were him. Imagine my surprise when you turned—”

The man palmed his weapon in a move so fast Riley didn’t have time to blink. Morrow aimed the gun at him. Riley's street training didn't allow him to freeze, he just dove behind the nearest tree as the gun cracked.

The bullet pinged off the large trunk, sending debris stinging against his face. "Hey! I'm one of the good guys! What are you doing?" Another bullet zipped past him and he raised his own rifle to his shoulder once again. "Stop shooting! I'm not trying to hurt you!" He peered around the rock, his blood pumping. His eyes met Morrow's and the man glared at him for another few seconds before he raised his weapon once again to aim it at Riley's face.

Riley pulled back just as another pop sounded then he heard the engine of the SUV roar to life.

Riley rose to his feet once again and watched the agent drive away while his heart thundered in his ears. Why had Agent Morrow reacted that way? Had he not heard him calling out to him? Of course he'd heard and *still* opened fire. His aim had been deliberate. Close shots that meant business. If the look in his eyes meant anything, Jake Morrow wasn't lost and he definitely didn't want to be found.

Riley reached for his cell phone, checked that he had a signal, and went to the news website. The number he'd seen on the television last night regarding reporting tips for Jake Morrow sightings was on the home page. He tapped the number and lifted his phone to his ear.

FBI Special Agent Harper Prentiss lowered her feet from her desk and leaned forward, her attention totally focused on what she was hearing. She'd been about to walk out the door to head home for the evening when the call had come through. Could this finally be the tip they were waiting for? "Tell me again. I want to make sure I didn't miss anything." And that his story didn't change.

The man on the other side of the conversation had identified himself as Riley Martelli and said he'd spotted Jake Morrow in Drum Creek, Colorado. Skepticism was her first reaction. They'd had so many bogus tips that her head hadn't stopped spinning with all the information she'd had to sift through. But the more this guy talked, the more she wondered if he'd really seen Jake.

He repeated the story word for word. The details didn't change. Nothing left out, nothing added.

They had to check it out.

"Hold on a second."

"Sure."

She did a quick Google search. It was about a ten-hour drive to Drum Creek. If they left within the hour, they'd have time for a couple of hours of sleep before jumping on the case. She pondered taking the choppers, but they'd need their vehicles for the dogs.

Then again, she wanted to get there before too much time passed and Jake had a chance to move on. Or, there was another option. One that made the most logistical sense. "All right, I'll tell you what. If I take a chopper, I can be there within a couple of hours. The others drive up with the vehicles and meet me there, but at least I can start searching."

"No sense in hurrying," Riley Martelli answered. "You're going to want to start your search where I last saw him, I'm sure. There's no searching in the dark. Not in that area, trust me."

"Give me the location."

"Rocky Mountain National Park. It's about an hour and forty minutes from Denver and about fifteen minutes from Drum Creek. It's got tons of camping areas, lakes and other great hiding places. I repeat, you won't find him in the dark."

Harper bit her lip, her frustration raging. She didn't want to have to wait until morning to start looking for Jake, but apparently she wasn't going to have a choice. They could chopper in lights and other equipment, but that was still risky. They could miss something important on the fringes of the light.

No, they'd have to start the search at dawn. "All right, we can be there first thing in the morning. Can you recommend a place to stay that can accommodate six team members and six dogs?"

"Sure. There's a hotel in downtown Drum Creek. I'm staying there right now. The owner is a friend of mine. What do you need? Six rooms?"

"Yes." Harper worried her bottom lip with her teeth. They had to be careful how they approached this. They still didn't know what they were dealing with. Was Special Agent Morrow an agent in need of help or was he a double agent, actually working for the very mafia kingpin they'd been trying to put away for months now? She just didn't know. But she was going to find out.

"Keep this confidential, will you? We're going to make a big enough splash with our vehicles and the dogs, but if you can help us fly as far under the radar as possible, that would be great."

Keeping the press and the public unaware of their classified missions was the only way to ensure the success of the team. However, with the dogs, the handlers had to be identifiable in certain situations so the FBI provided a variety of uniforms and gear for different occasions. Max West, their team leader, would have to figure out the best option for this situation.

"I'll do my best and I'll reserve the rooms for you," the bounty hunter was saying. "Like I said, the guy who owns the hotel and works the early morning desk is a friend of mine. He can keep his mouth shut—and if you park in the back, your vehicles won't be seen from the main road."

"Perfect."

"I'll meet you in the lobby at 5:30 sharp. Sunrise is around 5:45. If we get out of town and head into the park early, there won't be a lot of traffic or inquiries."

"Good. Our vehicles are black Suburbans. No flashy logos or anything." But the dogs would attract attention. They gathered stares wherever they went. She sighed. Well, they could only do their best.

"Sounds good."

"Thank you, Mr. Martelli."

"Call me Riley."

"All right, Riley, see you in the morning."

She hung up and sent an email to her team. She was a member of the elite FBI Tactical K-9 Unit. While the FBI started its K-9 program many years ago, the Tactical K-9 Unit was started by the agency ten years ago in response to the increased levels of terrorism haunting the country. They ultimately answered to the FBI Director, but her team was special in that they had very little micromanaging from above. They were good at their jobs and the director knew it. He left them alone, only requiring debriefs as necessary from their team leader.

Harper's computer dinged as the responses came in. Good, everyone would be ready to leave by five this afternoon. They'd drive to Colorado, check into the hotel, sleep a couple of hours and be ready to roll by 5:30 a.m. She shut the laptop and placed it in her bag.

They had to find Jake. He'd disappeared in the shootout with the Dupree kingpin and his uncle, Angus Dupree, in Los Angeles, California. Jake's Malinois, Buddy, was injured in the shootout and was slowly recovering. Unfortunately, as smart as he was, he couldn't talk and tell them what happened or where his partner went. It was up to Jake's team to find him and bring him home.

Or bring him to justice.

Riley glanced at his watch. 5:28. On any other morning, it would be too early for the motel to have breakfast ready, but he had requested that pastries and juice be available for the team. Since the two of them were friends, the manager had been happy to oblige and had even added scrambled eggs and bacon to the spread. Special agents milled around the buffet, their expressions solemn, determined and ready for anything. Each one had a highly trained, working dog. He didn't see how they would be able to fly under the radar, but working in the early morning hours while most people still slept or late into the evening would help.

His gaze moved back to the woman who had captured his interest the moment she'd entered the breakfast area. She was one of two females in the group and he assumed she was the one he'd spoken to on the phone yesterday.

Harper Prentiss. He liked her name and thought it suited her. She looked to be in her late twenties. Her dark hair was cut short, but in a style that flattered her face. Her blue eyes had locked with his just moments before and he figured she'd be heading his way after she finished her bagel. He swallowed another sip of coffee. He hadn't expected her to be so pretty.

Special Agent Prentiss took her last bite and walked over. Her German shepherd stayed at her heel and sat when Harper stopped in front of him. "Riley Martelli?"

He stood and held out a hand. "Yes, ma'am."

"You're here early."

"I like to be prepared."

A faint smile curved her lips and small creases formed at the corners of her eyes. "Thank you for reserving the rooms. We needed them by the time we got here."

"Hope you got some rest."

"A few hours, but we're used to going without when we have to." She looked around and he noticed the others clearing their trash. Her gaze landed back on his. "We'll be ready to roll in just a few minutes."

"All right. Your vehicles look like they'll hold up to the rugged terrain."

"They will." She paused. "This is an afterthought, but I don't suppose you got a picture of the guy you saw?"

"Nope, but his face has been plastered all over the news and that was the guy."

"And he shot at you," she murmured.

"He did. And kept shooting even after I identified myself with my arms up and my weapon held over my head. Trust me, he wasn't interested in being helped. The bullets he fired weren't warning shots. They were way too close for comfort. If he could have killed me, he would have. He wanted me dead."

She frowned and exchanged a look of concern with the man on her left. He'd been listening to the exchange and now he nodded and stood. "Guys? Let's do a quick introduction and get going. You all about ready?"

A chorus of yeses answered him. One by one, each team member stepped up to introduce himself and his partner. A tall, green-eyed agent with short blond hair held out a hand. "I'm Leo Gallagher." He gestured to the chocolate Lab at his side. "This is True. Nice to meet you."

Riley nodded. Next was the other pretty woman on the team. "Julianne Martinez and Thunder." The foxhound's ears twitched at his name and he looked up at her. She patted his head and they followed Leo out the door.

"Max West." He was the one who'd stood and told them all to head out. Max was tall with short blond hair and blue eyes. He had a wicked-looking scar on his left cheek and Riley couldn't help but wonder what had happened. "This is Opal."

Riley shook his hand.

Harper leaned over as Max headed out the door. "Max is the boss," she whispered. "Everything goes through him."

"Right."

All of the agents were friendly enough, but the walls were there. Riley didn't take it personally. He'd been in law enforcement once upon a time so he got it. They didn't know anything about him. He could be some thrill seeker who got his kicks by calling in false leads and making everyone jump through hoops. He'd have to prove himself, or at least prove he wasn't mistaken—or lying—about spotting Morrow.

Another tall, muscular man stepped up and held out a hand. "Ian Slade." He scratched the ears of the Belgian Malinois at his side. "This is King. Thanks for your help." He moved on toward the door.

"And last, but not least, I'm Zeke Morrow and this guy here is Cheetah." The Australian shepherd was a gorgeous animal. All of the dogs were.

"Morrow?" Riley asked.

"Jake's my brother."

"Okay, then. I hope we find him fast."

"That makes all of us." Zeke's lips flattened and he walked out the door.

Harper sighed and met Riley's gaze. "He's having a hard time."

"I'm sure," Riley murmured.

"Now that you've met the team, we can get going. We're all ready to find Jake and put this case to bed. Why don't you ride with me? Star here has her own area in the vehicle."

He nodded and followed her out the door to climb into the passenger seat. Star slipped into the back and Harper slid into the driver's seat.

Leo and True walked over. "Is there room for us? There's no reason to take all the vehicles."

"Of course. There's room for True in there with Star for this ride. It's not that long a trip according to the GPS." They climbed in and True settled into the designated area with Star. The custom-designed vehicle came with a climate-controlled spot where the dogs had been trained to ride.

The other agents and dogs dispersed themselves between two of the other vehicles. Harper cranked the Chevy and pulled out of the hotel parking lot.

For the next twenty minutes, the three of them made small talk and he learned Harper had graduated from high school and then gone straight into the army. "You didn't want to make a career of it?"

"Nope, just wanted my degree in Criminal Justice. As soon as I had that and the loans paid off I got out and applied to the FBI. I had pretty decent grades in high school, but nothing that stood out so the army made sense for me. My dad took off when I was little and my mom found her comfort at the bottom of a bottle and eventually died from alcohol poisoning." She slid a glance at him. "My options were pretty limited. I just knew I didn't want to be like either of my parents."

"You're pretty open about all that."

She shrugged and smiled. "I've come to grips with it. Every once in a while I'll get asked to do a demonstration at a school and instead of just making it all about the dog, I decided that sharing about my past might help someone make better decisions for their future. Kind of a 'you might have it bad right now at home, but that doesn't have to define your future' thing."

Riley found himself fascinated by Harper after that short snippet. Fascinated and wanting to know more about her. Which made him leery. He'd just met her so why did she hold such attraction for him? "Where'd you grow up?" he asked before he could bite his tongue on the question.

"In San Diego."

"Any brothers and sisters?"

"No, I'm an only child." Her lips twisted. "I was kind of sad about it when I was younger, but all things considered, it was better that way." She shot him a glance. "What about you?"

His heart aching, he cleared his throat. "I had a sister. She was killed two months ago by Van Blackman, the guy I'm chasing."

She snapped her head around to look at him then jerked her gaze back to the road. He heard Leo let out a slow breath in the backseat.

"I'm sorry," Harper said softly.

Leo reached forward and patted him on the shoulder. "I am, too."

"Thanks. She's the reason I'm in Drum Creek. I'm originally from Denver, but I got word that my sister's killer was spotted around this vicinity so headed over the night before last. I thought I saw Van coming out of the general store and followed him. Turned out to be your guy. He looks real similar to Jake Morrow—big build, a few inches over six feet, same hair color..." He shrugged. "Dress them in practically identical clothing and they could almost pass for twins."

"You left out some of the story last night."

He shrugged. "The parts I left out weren't important at the time." He pointed. "Turn here."

She did and followed the dirt path around the lake and to a small area where he directed her to park. "This is where I parked the other day or I would have been able to follow him out of the park. I'm familiar with this area so knew he wasn't going far once he got past that boulder up there. Unfortunately, he drove and was able to get away." The trees swayed in the summer breeze and right now, the area looked like something one would see on a postcard. Harper shut off the engine and the others behind her did the same.

Once they were all out of the vehicles, they let the dogs take care of business then Harper pulled a baseball cap from a plastic bag and held it in front of Star's nose. The dog got a good whiff and Harper replaced the hat in the bag then turned to Riley. "I see what you mean about not searching at night. The terrain is rugged. It would be pitch-black at night. Even with large lights and other equipment brought in to help with the search, there'd be no guarantee you wouldn't miss something."

"Exactly."

"All right, lead the way."

Riley made his way down the trail he'd followed Morrow on yesterday just before lunch. The others fell into step behind him, fanning out, letting their animals sniff and search along the way.

Riley finally reached the area where he'd seen Morrow. "Tell the others to stay back. You don't want to compromise the scene."

She lifted a brow but turned and did as he asked. The others stopped.

"Sorry," he said. "I guess you know how to work a scene."

"We do."

She opened the bag and held the hat out to her shepherd again. After she got a whiff, the dog stepped forward, nose to the ground, then in the air. Star went a little ways then sat and gave a low bark right next to the remains of the small campfire. She seemed almost disappointed that it had been so easy and not a challenge to her superior skills.

Special Agent Harper Prentiss turned those electric blue eyes on him. "Well, well, what do you know?" She turned to the others. "He was here."

"Good," Riley said. "Because I really need that reward money."

Harper blinked in surprise, but didn't pursue the matter. "Okay. Well then, I guess we'll have to see that you get it. Hopefully, between the seven of us, we'll pinpoint Jake's location before nightfall. And you'll get your reward money."

Riley grimaced. He'd sounded very greedy but he'd have to explain his reasons for his desperation later. He grasped her arm in a gentle grip. "I don't mind staying with you and helping guide you in this area, but you need to know something."

"What?"

"Your danger level is going to skyrocket if you hang around me."

"Because…?"

"Van Blackman's not only my sister's killer, he's vowed to kill me, too."

TWO

Harper's eyes widened. "Why is he gunning for you?"

"Blackman knows I won't rest until he's either in prison or dead. And he knows I'm the one that's most determined to see that one of those two things happen. He's just as insistent that they won't. He sent me a note saying that if I continued to come after him, he'd see me dead, but if I let him go, he'd disappear and I'd never hear from him again."

"I see. And you can't let him go."

"That's not even on the radar. And not just because he killed my sister and shot my nephew, although that's a huge part of it."

"What's the other part?" she asked.

Riley's jaw clenched and his brown eyes flashed. "He'll do it again if he isn't stopped."

"Yeah." She drew in a breath. "All right, thanks for the warning. I'll talk to Max, but I have a feeling he'll say that we'll take our chances. You know this area and we need someone that can help guide us." She paused. "Why is he hanging around here? Why doesn't he just leave?"

Riley shook his head. "Believe me, I've asked myself that same question. He has a vehicle, but I'm not sure how much money he has. The only thing I can figure is that he knows Denver and the park like the back of his hand. He's comfortable here. He also knows that if he leaves, I'll be right behind him. I think he's tired of running and just wants to see me dead so he can get on with his life."

She nodded slowly. "Makes sense."

"Yeah. It actually makes things easier for me, believe it or not." He turned to walk toward Ian and she frowned while she stared at the bounty hunter's broad back. His blunt statement that he needed the reward money bothered her. Sure, a hundred grand was a lot of money, a fortune for some people. But still…

Disappointment streaked through her. She didn't know why she expected Riley to be different. But she did. What was it that made her want to hold him to a higher standard? She shook her head.

Then wariness flowed through her as another thought surfaced. Could this be some sort of a setup? A distraction from what they needed to be focused on? According to Star, Jake had definitely been in the area—and recently. But what if Riley was working with Morrow? Could he be a part of the Dupree crime family himself? She pulled her phone from the clip on her belt and sent a text to Dylan O'Leary: Background on Riley Martelli needed ASAP. Dylan was the unit's technical guru. Based in Billings, Montana, he kept the unit running smoothly. He could do anything with a computer and find just about any information needed.

She discreetly snapped a picture of Riley while he was talking with Ian then sent that to Dylan as well.

On it.

She smiled at his immediate response and knew she'd have everything she needed before too long. She turned her attention back to Riley. He was looking her way and motioned her over.

Harper clipped her phone back to her belt and went to see what they'd found. Star stayed at her side.

"Where are we?"

Ian nodded to a small area on the ground. "Someone built a fire here and Star says it was Jake."

"He was camping out here." It wasn't a question.

"Maybe, but when I followed him to this spot, he didn't have any kind of camping gear set up," Riley replied. "He simply started a fire."

Harper frowned. "But why?"

"Maybe he was bored and passing the time. Who knows?"

Harper squatted next to the doused fire. "Or he was burning something he didn't want anyone else to see." She picked up a small stick and separated the ashes. Bits of white paper were noticeable. "A note?"

"Again…maybe," Riley responded.

"Some of the pieces aren't completely burned and have writing on them." She glanced up at him. "You might have had him running before he could finish the job." Using the stick, she managed to flip one of the larger pieces of paper. "Potter," she said, then gasped. "Hey, this could have something to do with Penny."

"Who's Penny?" Riley asked.

"The mother of Jake Morrow's child."

"Whoa."

"Yeah." Harper sighed and stood. "We've been looking for her and her son, Kevin, because we figure she can lead us to Jake. He was spotted at her home near Billings just a few days ago, but ran when we got there."

"Wait a minute, if he was at her house—and here at the national park—then he's definitely not a captive of the Dupree family. And if he's not a captive and needs help—because he sure didn't want mine yesterday—then what's he doing? Why isn't he reaching out to you?"

"We've pondered all of that, of course, but we just don't know." She had her thoughts, but kept them to herself for now. "He's not a captive," Harper said. "That much we *do* know." The question was, was he a double agent? As much as she didn't want to believe it, she couldn't help but think he might be working for the Duprees. She just couldn't figure out any other reason for Jake to be acting the way he was.

Even if he was worried about Penny and needed to find her, all he had to do was ask and they'd all join in the search for her. As a team. But he was working alone and seemed to want to keep it that way.

"So, like you said, you stay on her trail and let her lead you to Morrow—or in this case, let Morrow come to you if you catch up with Penny first," Riley mused.

"That's the plan."

"All right," Max said. He motioned for the

team to gather round. "Let's get this area processed. We'll do it ourselves and make sure it's done right." They retrieved the necessary supplies from the vehicles, moved in and got busy working on it.

Harper's phone buzzed and she pulled it up to look at the screen.

A message from Dylan. *Still working on your request, but this anonymous text just came in and wanted to get it to you straightaway. Forwarding it now.*

She waited. The team had been receiving anonymous texts leading them to various places around the country. The person sending the texts seemed to want to help find Jake. However, remaining anonymous was obviously more important to the sender. And they were very skilled at making sure they stayed that way. Even Dylan hadn't been able to track the texts.

The buzz came again. *Find Morrow's toddler and find Jake. That simple.*

She resisted the urge to snort. Right...that simple. If only. Harper pondered the fact that Penny had run when all the trouble with Jake started and they had figured out that the missing agent was most likely looking for her. Only a month ago, they'd gone to Penny's house and had run into Jake doing the same thing. Only he'd bolted when he saw them. Which made no sense to her.

So if Jake was in the park, that was a good indication that Penny and her child were here as well. But where? And why Colorado? She glanced back at the pile of ashes then texted Dylan again. See if Penny has any connections here in Colorado, please. Let me know ASAP.

Sure thing.

Thanks. So how are the wedding plans progressing? Dylan was madly in love with Zara Fielding. Zara was a former team intern who was currently training at Quantico to become an agent. She was also Dylan's fiancée.

Beautifully. Haven't talked to her in a couple of days so I'm going through withdrawal. If you talk to her, tell her to call me.

Will do.

TTYL.

"Hey guys," she called, "we've gotten another anonymous text." The others gathered around her and she shared the message.

"I'd really like to know who's sending these," Ian muttered.

"Dylan will figure it out eventually. Let's finish up here and see what the lab can come up with."

For the next three hours, they worked the scene, but Morrow was obviously long gone and nothing else turned up that she would consider helpful. Finally, Harper sighed and walked over to Max. "I think we're done here, what do you think?"

"I think you're right." He motioned the others over. When everyone was within hearing distance, he asked, "Anyone else hungry? My breakfast wore off long ago."

Chimes of agreement rolled in and Harper looked at Riley. "Any place in town you can recommend?"

"Of course. The motel opens their restaurant for lunch. Then there's the Drum Creek Café that serves burgers, fries, shakes and salads. Or if you want something a bit fancier, there's Twilights right on the edge of town overlooking a small lake." His eyes held hers. "It's a great place for a date."

Ian had a coughing fit. Max snorted. Harper blinked and heat invaded her cheeks. "I don't need fancy since I don't do dates," she said. "The café works for me. What about you guys?"

They swallowed their mirth and nodded. Harper could almost see Ian biting holes in his tongue to keep from commenting. She shot him a warning glare. He grinned then turned to help gather their gear and together they hiked back to the vehicles. Riley walked with Max, the two of them talking. Max would fill her in later if it was something she needed to know.

But what was that comment about a date? Seriously?

Ian stepped over beside her and nudged her with a small grin. "It's a good place for a date," he drawled. "Wonder if he has anyone in mind?"

She slugged him in the arm and he laughed while he jogged ahead. At least he'd waited until he was out of Riley's earshot before he let loose with the teasing.

While she walked, Harper pushed Ian's ribbing aside and pondered her reaction to the good-looking bounty hunter. She admitted her attraction and questioned her sanity at the same time. She had no business letting herself be drawn to this man since she still had questions about his motives and whether or not he could be working with Jake. She didn't really *think* so, but…

Harper gave herself a mental shake and held the door for Star to hop in. She was *not* attracted to him. There.

Riley settled into the passenger seat with Leo

and True behind them again. Once Harper was in the driver's seat and headed down the road, she glanced at her handsome passenger. "Are you going to eat with us?"

"No. I have something I need to take care of."

"What's that?"

He shrugged. "Just...something. Personal stuff."

She raised a brow but kept silent. It was none of her business after all. A short time later, she pulled in front of the café and Riley opened his door. He turned back to her. "Let me know if there's anything else I can do to help."

"I will. Thank you for leading us out there today."

"You're welcome." He glanced at his watch. "I've got to get going." He shifted then rubbed a hand over his chin. "Will you let me know if I can collect the reward money?"

Harper frowned. "Sure. If we find Jake here due to your call, we'll get your money to you."

He flushed. "I know I sound money-hungry. It's not that, it's just my—"

"It's really not my business. I'll be in touch."

Riley nodded then exhaled sharply. "Right. Thanks." He climbed out and shut the door. She watched him walk to his car and sighed. Why had she interrupted him?

Because his *great place for a date* comment

still rang in her ears. And because she didn't think she'd mind one bit going on a date with him.

Even though she didn't date. And even though she might want to. No, she didn't. Because she was *not* attracted to him, she reminded herself. She had a job to do. Period.

A rap on her window made her jump. When she turned, Max was waiting for her. She lowered the window. "You coming?" he asked.

She turned to see Riley pull away from the parking lot and made up her mind. "I want to check on something first if that's all right."

He frowned. "What?"

"I'm going to follow him. I want to see where he's going. I'm still not a hundred percent convinced he's not somehow working with Jake."

Max gave a slow nod. "Might not be a bad idea. You want some backup?"

"Not yet. I'll call if I need you."

Riley cruised down I-70 toward Denver and thought about the morning. He was hungry but would get something in the hospital cafeteria. His need to see his nephew ate at him. And he needed an update from the doctors.

But he couldn't help the groan that slipped from his throat. "A great place for a date? Really?" His eyes had locked on Harper's and that was what he'd thought. And that was what had come out of his mouth. He shook his head. He wasn't usually so free with his words. But there was just something about her…

He sighed.

He didn't need to focus on that. Instead, he needed to keep his attention on his nephew and helping him heal. A budding attraction for the pretty FBI agent would only distract him and neither he nor his nephew needed that right now. Priorities, he reminded himself. Priorities.

An hour and forty-five minutes later, he arrived in Denver and pulled into the hospital parking lot. He turned the vehicle off and simply sat there a moment. He wanted to pray, to beg God for guidance, money and healing for his nephew, but…

He wanted to believe that God was who He said He was. But so much had happened in the last year that made him question his faith. Made him wonder if he believed in a God who either wasn't all-powerful or just didn't really care about what was going on with him personally. He pushed out of his truck. No time to ponder the heavy stuff. Asher was waiting for him.

Riley walked through the doors of the hospital. He made his way to Asher's floor and headed for the child's room. As he passed the nursing station, the men and women greeted him. "Glad to see you back. Asher's been asking for you. His teacher is here, too."

"Thanks."

He opened the door and found his mother sitting in the chair she'd occupied since his sister's death and Asher's admittance into the hospital. Her needles clicked softly and a ball of yarn spilled from the bag next to her chair. A dark haired, dark-eyed woman sat on the edge of Asher's bed. The little guy held a card in his hand and others spilled over his lap and the smile on his face was worth more than gold.

"Hi, I didn't realize he had company," Riley said as he leaned over and kissed the top of his mother's head.

"I'm Beth Smith," the woman said. "I was Asher's first grade teacher last year. I heard about what happened and about two weeks ago rounded up his classmates and friends. We had a card-making party for Asher and I was very excited to be able to bring them to him today."

Riley shook her hand. "That's very kind."

"I miss them, Uncle Riley."

He smoothed the child's hair from his forehead. "I know you do, buddy. Maybe some of them can come see you soon since you're feeling better."

"That would be awesome."

Riley smiled at the enthusiasm.

"Can I have a puppy, too?"

"A puppy?"

Asher turned those thick-lashed blue eyes on him. "I really think I need a puppy. It can keep me company and make me feel like laughing again."

Mrs. Smith gasped and Riley saw tears in her eyes before she looked away.

His heart clenched and he found it hard to draw in breath around the grief that filled him. He cleared his throat. "We'll have to see. I'm not making any promises, but we'll talk about it when you get out of the hospital. Deal?"

"Deal."

And Riley was going to do whatever it took to make sure Asher felt like laughing again.

"Hey, you know what?" he said.

"What?"

"I met someone who has a dog. You want me to ask her to bring it up here?"

Asher's eyes widened. "Today?"

"Probably not today, but maybe soon?"

"Yes, please, Uncle Riley. That would be double awesome!"

"Okay, then."

"What kind of dog?" he asked.

"She's a police dog. She helps sniff out the bad guys."

"Wow," Asher breathed.

"A police dog?" Mrs. Smith asked.

Riley nodded. "Yes."

"I have a group of summer campers who are thinking about going into law enforcement. Their favorite topic has been K-9s and their work with the different areas of law enforcement."

"Where are you doing the camp?"

"Out at the national park. We're in the part where they have cabins and decent restroom facilities."

"Roughing it, huh?"

She laughed. "Not too bad."

"I wish I could go to camp," Asher said softly.

Riley squeezed the boy's shoulder. "Let's aim for next summer, okay?"

Asher nodded. "Where I can go and learn about being a police officer so I can catch the bad guys?"

"Sure."

Mrs. Smith kissed Asher's cheek and rose. "Well, I suppose I need to say my goodbyes." She gathered her purse and walked toward the door. "I only managed to slip away from the camp for a short time and need to get back. Asher, I'll check back in on you soon."

Asher waved. "Bye, Mrs. Smith. Thank you for coming to see me."

"You're welcome, sweetheart." She smiled and Asher's lids drooped. The visit had tired him out. Riley said one more goodbye to Mrs. Smith then sat with Asher and held him until he dozed off. It didn't take long. He slid off the bed and turned to his mother who still worked with the needle and yarn. "Another blanket?"

"Yes." She looked up and gave him a weary smile. "It keeps me busy and helps me think. And besides, they're selling pretty well at the little consignment store Sheila runs. She keeps asking for more."

Sheila, his mother's best friend, worked at a consignment store in downtown Denver. She'd encouraged his mother to let her sell some of her items and to everyone's surprise, it had turned into a full-time job keeping up with the demand.

"Now that we're alone, is there any change? Any updates?" His gaze went back to Asher, who was dwarfed by the large bed. The boy appeared to be sleeping comfortably.

His mother laid her knitting aside and rubbed her eyes. "No, son, you know nothing's going to change without the surgery. The doctor said he's strong enough for it now—he's recovered nicely from the bullet in his shoulder and now they just need to get in and get the other one out."

He nodded. Of course he knew that, but each day that went by, he hoped. Hoped his nephew's spine would heal on its own, that he would sit up in the bed, whole and happy again. Riley vaguely wondered how long it took for hope to finally dry up. "I wish Dad was here."

Tears sprang to his mother's eyes and Riley wished he'd kept his mouth shut. His father had passed away two years ago after a short battle with brain cancer.

She swiped a stray tear. "I do, too, son. Are you any closer to catching Van?" she asked.

He rubbed his eyes. "Yes. I think so. I have a good idea where to look for him now." He fell silent for a moment. "That was nice of Mrs. Smith to drop by."

"Very nice. Asher looked forward to it all morning."

Riley reached for her hand and held it, noticing the texture of her still-smooth skin, feeling the warmth of her fingers. A hand that had wiped his tears and cleaned his little boy knees and elbows, had cradled him in her arms when his prom date had stood him up. He was a man who still wanted—if not needed—his mother and her comfort. He wondered if he should be ashamed to admit that. "How are you feeling? Are you taking your medicine?"

"I am." She had a heart condition that required daily medication. One reason she felt she couldn't handle full custody of Asher and why Riley had agreed to be the one to take him should anything happen to his sister. He'd never thought he would be in the position he now found himself. He swallowed and stepped next to the child to run a hand over Asher's sweet face. The boy opened his eyes.

And smiled. "You're still here."

Riley's heart tripped over itself at the love and trust reflected there. He leaned closer and pressed a kiss to Asher's forehead. "Sure I am. How are you doing, Champ?"

"I want to go outside and play."

Riley's throat tightened on the tears that wanted to flow on behalf of the little boy he loved so much. "Soon, Asher. I sure hope you can do that soon."

"Me, too."

"Maybe we can get a wheelchair and roll you outside in a little while."

"Okay." Asher closed his eyes again then opened them when the door opened and the doctor walked in. The boy reached for Riley's hand and held on but there was no fear in his blue eyes. For that Riley was grateful. He'd promised Asher that everyone in the hospital was there to help him walk again and Asher believed him. For now.

The doctor started to speak and Riley fingered one of the tubes running out of the little guy's body. Fresh fury rocked him. He drew in a deep breath. *God, where are You? Where were You? Why didn't You protect them?*

THREE

Harper frowned as she waited on Riley to come back out of the room he'd entered.

They were on the pediatric floor and Harper would admit, once she realized he was heading for the hospital, she'd thought he might be meeting a woman who worked there. A girlfriend nurse or doctor. Then she wondered why that was her first thought. She finally admitted it was because she wanted to know if there was someone special in his life. She grimaced. Why did it matter? It was not like she wanted him to act on his subtle hint about going to the restaurant on a date. Not with her, anyway. Did she?

She did.

And she didn't.

She loved her job and knew she was good at it, but deep down, in a place she would only admit to herself, she wanted more. But she was afraid she just wasn't meant to have a family of her own. And right now wasn't the time to think about it. Conflicted, she pushed the thoughts away and focused on the reason she was there.

Once they'd arrived on the floor, the fact that everyone greeted Riley warmly seemed to support the theory that he was a regular visitor. But he hadn't spoken to any of the women there other than to offer a brief wave and a smile. He'd gone into one of the rooms followed by the doctor shortly thereafter. Her curiosity ramped up into high gear.

But one thing was settled. He definitely wasn't meeting Jake Morrow. So who? The woman who'd walked out wiping tears from her cheeks? She definitely looked like someone who might be Riley's type. Pretty, with a sweet smile she'd shot at the nursing station as she'd passed by.

Harper stayed where she could see the door and waited. Ten minutes later, her patience paid off. The doctor stepped out and she waited for him to walk her way. "Excuse me?"

He stopped. "Yes?" He looked to be in his midforties and was a good-looking guy with kind green eyes.

Harper flashed her badge. "I'm investigating a case. Do you know Riley Martelli?"

"Of course. He's Asher's uncle. A better guy you'll never meet."

The glowing endorsement eased her nerves a bit. "That's good to hear. And your patient is Asher?"

The kind eyes hardened. "Yes."

"Can you tell me what happened to him?"

"No. HIPAA laws and all that." Harper frowned and the doc lifted a brow. "But it was all over the news. You didn't see it?"

"I'm not from around here. Can you fill me in?"

He hesitated and shrugged. "I can tell you what was on the news. Asher caught two bullets when a stalker went after his mother."

Harper gasped. "That's horrible." Even though she'd seen a lot of awful in her line of work, she would never become numb to murder.

He nodded. "Charlotte, Asher's mother, died almost instantly with a bullet that went through her heart. Asher pulled through. One of the bullets is lodged very near his spine and he needs some pretty tricky surgery to remove it. The one that went through his shoulder did some damage, but nothing major."

"But he'll be all right?"

"He's already pretty well recovered from that one. Until we can get the bullet from his back, though, he won't be able to walk. And yes, all of that was on the news—well, on television in a press conference, I guess you would say. After Charlotte was killed, her mother went on television and told the story. She then begged people to be on the lookout for Van Blackman and to call the police if he was spotted."

"Did it help? Her plea?"

The doctor shrugged. "They got some leads but nothing that panned out." His nostrils flared. "And so he's walking around a free man while that little boy now has no mother and can't get out of that bed." His eyes flashed in fury at the injustice and Harper tried to process the words and push aside her shock.

"When is he supposed to have the surgery?" she asked.

"We've been waiting for him to heal enough to handle it. When he first got here, we didn't think he was going to make it, but he's pulled through like a champ." He smiled proudly. "In fact, that's his new nickname around here. Champ. We're still waiting to see when we can schedule the surgery."

"Doctor? Special Agent Prentiss?"

She froze and grimaced. Busted. She turned to find Riley staring at her. "I told you to call me Harper."

He raised a brow. "Harper. What are you doing here?"

She opened her mouth then shut it. What could she say?

His hands went to his hips and he frowned. "Did you follow me?"

"Yes."

"But...why?"

Harper glanced at the doctor who looked decidedly uncomfortable. She offered him a small smile. "Thank you."

"Sure." He escaped quickly.

Harper looked back at the glowering Riley. "I don't blame you for being mad. I just had to make sure you weren't meeting with Jake Morrow."

"Meeting with Ja—" He ran a hand through his reddish blond hair. "Why would I be meeting with the man who shot at me?"

He was either truly confused or an Oscar worthy performer. "I don't want to take you away from your nephew, but is there somewhere we can go to talk? When you're finished?" Her phone buzzed but she ignored it for the moment.

He stared at her a moment longer then shrugged. "Let me tell my mother and Asher what I'm doing. We can go down to the cafeteria and get a sandwich. I'm starving."

"Sure."

He started to walk away then turned back. "Hey, do you have Star with you?"

"Yes. She's in the car. Why?" She'd wanted to remain inconspicuous. Walking in with Star would have made her stand out like a sore thumb. The dog was fine in the temperature-controlled area of the vehicle.

"I'll tell you in a minute."

He was gone all of thirty seconds before he returned. "I was going to ask you to bring Star up to see Asher, but he's sleeping deeply. I don't want to disturb him."

"I'm happy to bring Star to see him. Just let me know when." They walked to the elevator. "So the doctor told me a little bit about what happened. He said Asher is your nephew."

"Yes."

"And Van Blackman, the man you mentioned, killed your sister. He shot your nephew, too." The doctor had given her the information, but she wanted to hear it from Riley. Guilt pierced her. She remembered him trying to tell her why he wanted the reward money and she'd cut him off.

"Yes. He stalked her for months before he finally snapped and opened fire on them in the grocery store parking lot. She died and I now have custody of Asher."

"I'm so sorry."

He nodded and a muscle ticked in his jaw. "I am, too."

Harper bit her lip. "Asher's why you need the money, isn't he?"

"Yeah. The medical bills are piling up. The insurance plan my sister had wasn't a very good one and Asher needs surgery. Extensive, expensive surgery. We've had a few people donate to a fund that was set up, but that money's running out and it's getting harder and harder to pay the bills."

Her heart went out to him. How awful.

Harper's phone rang again and this time she pulled it from the clip on her belt. "Excuse me. Why don't you get in line and get your food? Go ahead and eat if I'm not back in time."

"You want anything? You didn't have time to eat if you followed me here."

"Get me whatever you're having. I'm not picky."

"Chicken salad?"

"Sure, and don't wait on me to eat. I never know how long I'll be when I get on the phone with Dylan." She hit the button to answer the phone before it could go to voice mail. "Prentiss here."

"Harper, this is Dylan."

"What do you have?"

"Your guy, Riley Martelli, is clean. I couldn't

come up with anything that connected him with Jake Morrow or anyone else that would throw up red flags. He was actually a cop for several years before he became a bounty hunter."

"What? He never mentioned that." She cut her eyes to him as he stood at the counter placing his order. Yeah, she could see him in some form of law enforcement. He had that aura about him.

"Yep. A decorated officer, too."

"Why'd he quit?"

"I don't know. There's nothing in his record to indicate what made him change careers. Whatever the reason, he's still catching the bad guys and putting them away. I did find out that his sister was murdered—"

"I know that part. He told me."

"He told you she had a stalker? And that he has sole custody of his nephew?"

"Yes."

"All right, then. Let's move to Penny."

"What about her?"

"Nothing. Meaning I couldn't find anything that might connect her to Colorado. No relatives, no job, no credit card action."

Harper pressed her thumb to her forehead where the beginning of a headache gathered. "Which might be exactly why she came here. For the very fact there was nothing in her past or present to lead anyone to think she'd run here."

"True. What else do you need?"

"Nothing. I needed what you just gave me." The assurance that Riley was on the up and up being the most important piece of intel. She was rather surprised at the intense relief that flowed through her.

"Great. Then I've got one more thing for you."

"I'm ready."

"I just got off the phone with Max. We've got the evidence in house and will be going through it shortly."

"Keep me updated."

"Of course."

"Thanks, Dylan."

She hung up. The fact that the evidence was already back at headquarters amazed her although it really shouldn't. Their unit's resources by far surpassed anyone else's. By helicopter, the flight time was probably slightly over an hour. Which meant they should have more information about the evidence by dinnertime.

In the meantime, assuming she had Max's okay, she needed to see how Riley felt about striking a deal with the FBI.

FOUR

Riley finished off his sandwich and sweet tea then leaned back to watch Harper get started on hers. She'd settled into her chair and eyed his empty plate. "Guess you were hungry?"

"I know you told me not to wait, but I still feel guilty for finishing before you even sat down. Guess I was starved."

"I'm glad you went ahead and ate."

He munched an apple while he waited for her to eat then say whatever was on her mind. Halfway through her sandwich, she finally looked up. "Sorry, looks like I was hungry, too."

He fell silent, thinking. She got up to refill her drink and when she came back he caught her eye. "Why would you think I was working with Morrow?" he asked.

She sighed. "You were so focused on the money." A shrug. "I don't know. I thought maybe you were helping him somehow."

"What do you think now?"

"I think you need the money for Asher. I'm sorry I was so suspicious and so quick to judge. I guess I so rarely come across someone who isn't willing to do just about anything for money that I can't recognize someone who doesn't have dollar signs in his eyes."

"The dollar signs are there, just not for personal gain. Unless seeing my nephew walk again falls into that category." His eyes narrowed on her. "I'm guessing my background check came back clean?"

She huffed out a low laugh. "Yes, it did. It also revealed something interesting about you."

"That I was a cop?"

"Are you a mind reader, too?"

He shook his head with a small smile. "No, it's just common sense—and it's not a secret. A simple background check would reveal it."

It was. "So, why the career change?"

He sighed and shrugged. "For several reasons. There wasn't any dramatic thing that happened. No specific incident that compelled me to turn in my resignation, I just…got tired."

"Of?"

"Recycling the criminals."

"Oh."

"I would arrest someone and then see them back on the street a week later. I was like, what's the point? So I started thinking about what I could do that would really make a real difference."

"But you *were* making a difference. Just the very nature of your presence, in your uniform, would be a deterrent to some people thinking of committing a crime."

He nodded. "I know. I agree. Uniformed officers are important and I'm not knocking them or what they do. I'm just saying for me, personally, I wanted to do something a little different. And being a bounty hunter seemed to fit the bill."

She took another bite of the sandwich then ate a handful of chips. "Do you miss it?"

"I miss certain aspects of it. You know how it is. When you're a cop, you're a part of a team. A whole culture that you can only be a part of if you're wearing the badge. You know what I mean?"

"Yes, I do," she murmured.

"I miss that connection with the others. Bounty hunting can be a lonely profession."

"You think you'll ever go back?"

Riley paused then nodded. "Maybe. One day." He stood. "But right now I've got to focus on finding my sister's killer. I hope you find Morrow."

She held up a hand. "Wait, don't leave yet. Sit back down, please?"

Curious, he sank back into the chair. "What is it?"

"Do you think we could help each other?"

He lifted a brow. "What do you have in mind?"

"Morrow was last seen by you. No more tips have come in since yours. You know those woods and the mountains out there, don't you?"

He gave a slow nod. "I've been going camping there since I could walk. First with my dad and uncles then with friends. Certain areas of it anyway. Why?"

"I have a feeling Jake's hiding out there."

"Well, I know for a fact Blackman is out here somewhere. I had a tip that he'd been spotted in Drum Creek. I've made a lot of friends in Drum Creek over the years. The owner of the general store, Paul Nelson, and my dad were good friends. Paul called me yesterday and said he'd seen Blackman in the store and he'd bought camping supplies. Said he was going to be hanging around until his business was finished."

"What business?"

"Good question. I haven't really figured that out yet, but…" He shrugged. "Anyway, the national park is the only place around Drum Creek that one would need camping supplies so I'm going to search every last acre if that's what it takes."

Harper frowned. "That could take a long time."

He sighed. "The truth is, there are so many places to hide it would be like looking for a needle in a haystack. Same thing with your guy. It's going to take time."

"I realize that, but we have to do something. Sitting around waiting on leads to come in isn't an option. Not when we know there's a good possibility Jake is hiding nearby." She rubbed her forehead. "My question is why he's sticking around here when he knows he's been spotted. What is his purpose in staying unless he doesn't think he needs to leave? Or doesn't care that he's been seen?"

"He cared enough to shoot at me."

"What if he didn't believe you were who you said you were? What if he thought you were working with the men who kidnapped him?"

"I suppose that's a possibility," he conceded.

"The anonymous person sending the texts seemed to think Jake was looking for Penny."

He quirked a brow. "Is Penny here in Colorado?"

"Not that we know of. What we do know is that Jake's not going to come to us, so we're just going to have to go find him. If you'll help us comb that area and lead us to where he might find a hiding place, I'll do my best to make all of our resources available to you to help find your sister's killer. I'll have to have my boss okay that, of course, but I don't see why he wouldn't."

He studied her then looked away for a brief moment while he considered the idea. *All of her resources at his disposal*. That would be a huge help. He nodded and captured her gaze with his. "All right," he said and held out his hand. "If your boss agrees, I'm willing to go with that."

She shook his hand and the feel of her soft fingers within his grasp made him wonder if his heart would survive the deal.

Riley looked up from Harper's pretty blue eyes. If he stared into them for too long, she muddled his thoughts.

His gaze landed on a figure near the door and he froze for half a second then leaped to his feet.

Harper jerked. "What is it?"

"Van Blackman." He bolted from the table and the man spun on his heels to dart out the door.

He heard Harper give chase as well. "Blackman, stop!"

"Federal agent," Harper called. "Stop now!"

Blackman kept going. Riley pounded after him. What was he doing at the hospital? Had he come to do something to Asher? To finish him off? Fury nearly blinded him and threatened to steal his common sense and self-control. Riley didn't slow, but Blackman was fast. Van pushed past people in the hospital, grabbed one man and shoved him in front of Riley. Riley caught the elderly man on a stumble. "Sorry, sir. Are you all right?"

"I think so."

Riley made sure the gentleman had his balance, losing precious seconds of the chase while Blackman lunged out of the hospital exit.

Harper raced past him. Riley fell in behind her and together they dashed out into the hot Colorado sun and ran down the sidewalk. He rounded the corner just in time to see Van jump into a car and speed off.

"No!" Riley skidded to a stop and tried to see the license plate, but Blackman was already turning the corner. "No," he rasped as he caught his breath.

Harper had run farther than he, only now she was walking back toward him, speaking into her phone. "...green Ford. Four doors, older model. Heading south on Platte Street. Right." She stopped in front of him. "Are you okay?"

"Just mad he got away again. I can't believe

he showed up here. He's following me. He's doing his best to push my buttons." He drew in a deep breath. "I refuse to let him do that."

"Good. Let's get Blackman's picture to hospital security and ask them to keep an eye out for him. Especially when you're in the building."

"That's a good idea." Riley clenched his fingers into fists. "He waited until I saw him. Stood there and simply waited for me to look up. He wanted me to know he was there, watching."

"He's definitely taunting you if that's the case."

"It's the case." Riley rubbed a hand over his face and pictured him catching Van and pummeling him into oblivion. No, death would be too easy for the man. He wanted him in prison for the rest of his life where Riley would make sure he constantly reminded the man why he was there. He planned to make prison worse than death for Blackman.

An uncomfortable niggle at his conscience reminded him that it wasn't his place to extract revenge for his sister's murder. It was just his job to bring the man in.

Right. He had a feeling he was going to have to keep telling himself that over and over before he had Blackman in custody.

* * *

Harper sat on the bed in her hotel room back in Drum Creek and opened the laptop she was never without. She'd shed her gear and flexed her shoulders. The vest weighed quite a bit, but she refused to go without it when on duty. And right now, she wondered if she should even take it off at all.

Jake Morrow was an outlier. She had no idea what he might or might not do. If he would shoot at a man who'd clearly identified himself as trying to help him, he might decide he didn't want her—or the team's—help, either.

Her ankle knife and service weapon lay on top of the vest within easy reach should she need them.

Star lounged at the foot of the bed, her head on her paws, eyes following Harper's every move. Harper scratched her faithful partner's ears then logged in to the secure software that she had access to. She pulled up the profile of the man she'd been looking for. His blue eyes stared back at her and she desperately searched her memory for even just one good thing to remember about him. But the mental search turned up nothing. As it did every time.

She sighed and shut the laptop. Her father was gone from her life. He'd chosen to leave when she was four. Not only leave, but he'd apparently never looked back. So why did she care about where he was, what he was doing—and if he had other children? She'd made something of her life without his help and was proud of that fact.

Still, when she was honest with herself, she would admit the rejection hurt. And that made it hard to picture herself married with children. And while she was being honest, she would also admit it was what she wanted. A husband to love and who loved her. A house full of children and a couple of dogs.

She had Star, of course, and loved the animal, but she wanted a puppy, maybe even several puppies. She smiled at the image then frowned. There was no need to go down that emotional road. It was a dream that had very little chance of coming true. After all, where would she find someone who understood her profession? And not only understood it, but would be willing to put up with it?

Riley's face came to the forefront of her mind and she grimaced. She didn't need to think about Riley. Because if she did, she'd have to admit to the attraction she knew was there. Okay, she could admit it.

But the timing was all wrong. Pursuing a romance at this moment was not an option.

Her goal, first and foremost, was to find Jake Morrow.

Unfortunately, her mind wanted to investigate the attraction she'd just acknowledged.

Fine. She leaned back and closed her eyes, picturing the bounty hunter with the chocolate-colored eyes that could draw her in and make her want to stay.

Riley Martelli. How would she describe him?

He was a fighter, a survivor. She liked that about him. After all he'd been through with his nephew in the hospital and needing surgery, and his sister killed by a stalker, he pushed through his grief. Or allowed the grief to push *him*?

Maybe.

He was good-looking in a rugged sort of way, intelligent, loyal, compassionate. And loved fiercely and fully. And he'd lost greatly.

Compared to him, she didn't think she'd had it quite so bad. Her father may have left her, but at least he was still alive somewhere. *God, I'm struggling. Struggling with You, and with this case. I need Your help, and I almost don't even want to ask for it because part of me is simply afraid You're not listening.* But she knew better than that. God was there. He was real and He cared about what she was going through. She had to believe that no matter what.

She sighed and let her mind jump to Jake Morrow.

She'd never liked him all that much even though she'd admired his skills as an agent. He'd definitely been one of the best agents she'd worked with. But as a person, a man? Not so much.

One of her earlier encounters popped to the forefront of her mind. He'd pressed her to go out with him and when she'd refused, he'd continued to push until she'd told him in no uncertain terms that she wasn't interested. He'd laughed and backed off, hands held as though she were aiming a weapon at him. "Chill, Harper. Man, you're uptight, aren't you? Loosen up and live a little." His words had been light, but the look in his eye had stayed with her and she'd slept with her gun nearby for several weeks after that incident. But he'd left her alone, seemed to forget all about it, and they'd worked well together in spite of the incident.

She sent a group text to the team. Have any of you guys heard from Zara? I think Dylan's missing her. He said something about going through withdrawals earlier today.

Nope.

Nada.

Negative.

Each response made her frown, but Zara was in training at Quantico. The rigorous schedule didn't leave much room for anything else.

But surely she could send a text to her fiancé.

Harper sent the woman a text of her own.

Call Dylan. He misses you.

Her eyes grew heavy and she drifted.

Until she heard something at her door. The knob jiggled. Her adrenaline immediately spiked and she sat up. Star was already on the floor facing the door. She gave a low woof. Harper put a hand on the animal's neck. "Stay," she whispered. Star didn't move. Harper glanced at the bedside clock. She'd been asleep most of the night still dressed in yesterday's clothes. Now it was close to six in the morning.

And someone was lurking outside her door.

She slipped to the window and moved the curtain enough so she could see outside.

Nothing was visible in her line of sight. She wrapped her fingers tighter around the butt of her weapon and stood to the side of the door.

Her phone buzzed on the nightstand and she jerked, her heart pounding in her chest.

Star lunged at the door and barked. Harper spun back to pay attention. Someone was out there. But who? She strode to the end table, grabbed her phone, then sent both Ian and Riley a group text: Someone's at my door. Can you see who it is?

Looking now, came Riley's response.

Don't see anything, Ian's text read. Coming out of my room now.

Got my door open and don't see anything, Riley said.

Harper snapped Star's leash on her collar and, using the hem of her shirt, slowly opened the door. She pointed to the knob. "Find, girl." The German shepherd sniffed the area Harper indicated then bolted from the room. Harper kept a tight grip on the leash, stepped out and shut the door behind her.

Ian and Riley were already there.

"Nothing here," Ian said. He held the leash to King, the energetic Malinois. The dog was ready to work.

Star pulled at the leash, too. "Star says differently." She and Ian let the dogs have their lead. Harper, with Ian right beside her, followed the animals along the edge of the building, passing room after room. The men trailed behind her and she knew they had her back.

Star came to the end of the building and rounded the corner. Harper went more cautiously, gripping the leash with her left hand and her weapon with her right. She glanced at

Ian and he nodded. Star whined and headed for the bushes across the parking lot. King joined her. A man shot out from behind them.

"Federal agent! Stop!"

Ian gave the same command.

The fleeing figure, dressed in jeans and a short-sleeved black shirt, ignored them both and darted toward a dark pickup truck parked at the edge of the hotel asphalt lot. Star and King gave chase, but he threw himself behind the wheel and the engine roared to life.

Riley raced past her and reached for the passenger side door handle. The truck swerved, throwing him sideways. He lost his grip, hit the ground with a grunt and rolled. Ian flew past, chasing the truck.

"Riley!" Harper hurried to him. He drew himself up on all fours and shook his head. "Are you all right?" she gasped.

"Yes. I'm fine." He got to his feet and winced.

"Did you get the plate?" Harper asked.

"I got part of it, but I don't need it."

Ian jogged over to them. "I got it." He pulled his phone from the clip on his belt and tapped a message. "Sent it to Dylan. We'll know something soon enough."

"I know who it is," Riley said. He bolted for his truck. Harper ran after him.

"Who is it?"

"Van Blackman." He yanked open the door and threw himself into the driver's seat.

Harper ran around to the other side and jumped into the passenger seat. Star leaped up and settled herself in the middle as Riley was backing out of the parking spot.

"How do you know it was Blackman?" she asked. "It looked like Jake to me."

"And I'm telling you, they look very similar." He pulled out of the parking lot with a squeal of rubber on asphalt. Harper looked back to see two black SUVs in pursuit as well. Her teammates weren't convinced it wasn't Jake, either.

"Open the glove box and pull out the picture there."

She did. A man and a woman, who had to be his sister, and a young boy about four years old grinned at her.

"See the guy on the left holding Asher?"

"Oh. Yeah. Wow, there really is a resemblance."

"Exactly."

"So how do you know the guy in the truck is Blackman and not Morrow?" she asked.

"I saw his eyes. Their eyes are different colors. Van's are green. The guy I spotted in the park had blue eyes. Very blue eyes."

"That sounds like Jake for sure." She'd been

the recipient of his blue-eyed laser stare more than she cared to remember.

He drove with precision, knuckles white on the wheel, eyes scanning.

"Do you see him?" she asked.

"No. I'm just going in the direction he went." Riley slapped the wheel. "I wasn't fast enough."

"Keep driving and looking. We need a chopper," she muttered. "Should have brought one in and held on to it for times like this." She made a mental note to suggest it to Max when they got back.

Riley drove another few miles then sighed. A sound filled with defeat. "I guess he's gone."

"Looks like it. I'm sorry." Her heart broke for him. He was working so hard to find his sister's killer and each time it looked like he might succeed, he got slapped down. He made a three-point turn and headed back to the motel. Harper noted that the others passed them. "They're going to keep searching."

"Good, I hope they find him."

"He'll show up again when he's ready."

He fell silent and Harper let him have the moments with his thoughts. When he pulled back into the parking lot of the motel, they climbed out of his truck and Ian jogged over to them. "Julianne and Zeke are still chasing him. They'll be in touch if they find him."

Harper nodded and Ian looked at Riley. "You're positive that it was Blackman and not Morrow?"

Riley shot him a dark look. "I'm sure. He's following us…me."

"But why would he try to get in my room?" Harper asked.

Ian tucked his weapon away. "Might have just gotten the wrong room. After all, you guys are right next to each other."

"Maybe."

Ian shrugged. "Or he thought you had something that he needed."

"Like what?"

"I don't know but hopefully we'll find out once we catch up with him again," Riley said. His gaze was locked on the direction in which the man had fled. "He's headed toward the park," he murmured.

"Could be," Harper said.

"He's hiding out there."

"Along with Jake Morrow."

Riley nodded. "We'll find them."

She walked back to her room to shut the door and noticed a piece of paper just inside on the floor. A piece of tape held it faceup. She started to pick it up and stopped. She walked over and grabbed a pair of gloves from her bag and slid them on. Then she went back to the piece of paper and lifted it up. *Martelli is a walking dead man. Stay away from him if you don't want to end up like his sister.*

Her heart thudded.

"What is it?" Riley asked from behind her.

She held it up and let him read it. "Looks like you were right," she said. "It was Blackman. It also looks like he doesn't like us hanging out together." She held the letter by the edge. "Threatening a federal agent. Wow, this guy wants his grave dug deeper than six feet, doesn't he?"

Riley's jaw tightened and for a moment she thought she heard his molars grinding. He took a deep breath. "Well, that explains why he was at your door." He gave her a tight smile. "But this is rather encouraging in a weird sort of way."

"What do you mean?"

"He thinks we're after him." She lifted a brow and he went on. "He doesn't know you're really here because of Jake Morrow," he explained. "Blackman thinks you're here for him." He gave a low laugh. "Oh, this is perfect. He thinks we're working together to catch him—and it worries him. I like that." His smile slipped into a frown as he stared at the note. "I don't like this, though."

She nodded. "Sounds reasonable."

He planted his hands on his hips and shook his head. "This was stupid on his part. Hopefully stupid will eventually trip him up."

"It usually does. We just need to give him a little time to get careless."

"Yes. So what are you going to do with the note?"

"Send it to Dylan." She smiled. "He's one of ours back in Billings and can find out just about anything and everything, but even I don't think he'll get anything off of this. Then again, you never know. There's a piece of tape that was probably supposed to hold it on the door. Maybe there'll be a print on that." She walked into her room while Riley waited in the open door. From her black carry-on, she pulled an evidence bag and slipped the note inside. Once sealed, she placed it on the desk.

Her phone buzzed and she glanced at the screen. "It's Dylan." She lifted the device to her ear. "What are you doing there so late?"

"You know me. I never sleep until my work is done." He kept his voice light, but she heard something beneath. "What do you have for me?"

"I've got something off of those scraps of paper you sent in. Well, the lab got something. I volunteered to call and fill you in."

"Great. What is it?"

"The last name Potter was obvious."

"Right. We're going on the assumption it's Penny."

"Your assumption would be correct. Looks like the rest of it is an address. I ran what I could make out through the system and it came back with several possibilities, but there was one that caught my attention. It's an address that belongs to an old ski chalet that's not too far from Drum Creek."

"Give me the address."

He did and she typed it into her phone. "Thanks, we'll head that way as soon as I round up the team."

"Hope it pans out."

"Me, too."

"I got Ian's license plate number. Should have something on that in the next little while."

"Excellent. Even though we know who was driving, maybe the plate will lead us to him. I'm also sending you a note that I found in my room." She filled him in on their early morning adventure. "See if the lab can pull any prints if you don't mind."

"Of course. I'll be looking for it."

"And I'll be looking forward to hearing from you." She hesitated. "Hey…did Zara contact you?"

"Nope. But I'm sure she's fine. I hope anyway."

There it was again. That odd note in his voice she'd heard when she first answered.

"What does that mean? You hope?"

He sighed. "Just that I still haven't heard from her. I'm getting a little worried."

"Not calling or being in contact doesn't sound like her."

"It's not."

"Let me know if you don't hear something soon and I'll see what I can find out," she said.

"Great. I'll give her a couple of more days. I know things are pretty intense at Quantico right now."

"She'll call or text when she can."

"I know. Thanks, Harper."

"Anytime." She hung up and sent a group text to the others, asking them to gather in the lobby of the hotel in fifteen minutes.

Once they'd assembled, Max gave her a nod and Harper brought everyone up to date on the incident in the parking lot. She also gave them the address Dylan had provided. Max motioned for her to continue taking the lead. "We think Penny Potter could be staying there. If she is, then Jake's probably not far behind. Evidence and that anonymous text lends support to that theory. He could even be with her right now."

Julianne leaned forward. "Come on, Max, tell us what you think about Jake. You really think he'd turn traitor?"

Max rubbed his eyes. "We've talked about this, discussed it until we're blue in the face and I still don't know the answer. I'm in contact on a daily basis with the director and he's as concerned as we are about Jake. Unfortunately, at the present time, we just don't know what's going on with him." He exhaled roughly. "I don't want to believe the worst, but the fact that he shot at Riley who wanted to help him doesn't bode well in his favor."

No, it doesn't, Harper thought.

Their team captain cleared his throat. "Plus, Jake's been seen all over the country so we know he's not in Dupree's clutches, and yet he hasn't reported in to let anyone know he's safe. He also seems to be tracking Penny. I'm going to assume it's because she has his child—which I can understand, but to not call us for help? Something definitely isn't adding up. It goes against everything I want to believe, but it's certainly possible that Jake is a double agent. For now," he said slowly, "I think we need to treat Jake like he's acting—a criminal on the run."

Frowns appeared on the agents' faces and Max held up a hand before the protests could start. "I don't like it, either, but I'm telling you, be careful if he contacts you. Don't trust him. Until he can explain his actions, he's an agent gone bad and wanted by the FBI. But that's classified. The press will keep airing the cover story we've released to them. In the meantime, keep these suspicions under your hat."

Silence fell over the group and Harper's emotions stepped onto the roller coaster. As hard as it was to admit, she'd already come to the conclusion that Jake was a bad agent herself. "We need a chopper out here, Max. That's a lot of territory to cover and I think we need air support that can be at our fingertips in a moment's notice."

He nodded. "I've already thought of that. One is on standby about ten minutes away at an old private airstrip."

"Good. The next thing on our list should be finding Penny—and fast," she said. "For her sake."

The others nodded. She saw Riley rub a hand across his eyes.

Harper drew in a breath and let it out slowly. "Which means our next stop is the address I just gave you. Dylan got the results from the lab and sent me the address from the charred piece of paper. I looked it up on Google Maps—it's an old ski chalet not too far from here. We need to be smart and careful, there's a child involved here. Everyone ready?"

"Ready."

"All in."

"Let's find her."

Harper nodded. "Follow me."

FIVE

Riley waited until the others filed out with their dogs then touched Harper's shoulder to get her attention. Her tension translated itself into the rock-hard muscle beneath his palm. "I'm going, too."

"I'm not so sure that's a good idea."

"I won't get in the way, but I want to be there. Jake's my nephew's ticket to surgery. I know it sounds bloodthirsty and I don't mean it that way, but I just—"

"You're already getting credit for the tip, Riley. Don't worry about it."

"I'm coming."

Harper frowned. They were the last ones left in the lobby. "You're just going to follow me if I say no, aren't you?"

He shrugged.

She sighed. "Fine, but if you get in the way, I'll throw you in jail, understood?"

"Understood."

Harper settled Star into her spot in the vehicle and the dog quivered with the excitement of going to work. Riley could tell the canine was born for this kind of work. Harper climbed into the driver's seat as Riley finished buckling his seat belt.

They pulled out of the parking lot, staying behind one of the other agents. The powerful SUVs didn't have any trouble on the winding mountainous roads that took them back to Rocky Mountain National Park so it didn't take long to reach the ski chalet.

Riley wasn't as familiar with this area as he was with the place where he'd spotted Jake so he took in the surroundings with interest. Harper parked a good distance away, but he could see the house perched on the side of the mountain. It looked like one could simply walk out the back door and ski down the slope. Nice. "No cars out front, but there's a detached garage."

"We'll check it out." She turned to him. "Stay put. Please."

He nodded. "I promise."

Harper studied him for a moment and he wondered what she was thinking. Then she blinked and turned to let Star out. The dog jumped to the ground and sat, her eyes on Harper, tail wagging. "Just a minute, girl. Stay."

Ian and King approached as well as Max and Opal. "We don't need to go in too fast," Max told them. "If Jake's in there with Penny and the child, we need to approach with caution."

"I agree," Harper said. Riley silently added his agreement.

"Harper, you and I and the dogs will take the front. Ian, you and King take the back. Check the garage and let us know what you see. Let the others know we'll signal if we need help and to go ahead and put their earpieces in."

"You got it," Ian said.

Ian and King turned away to go tell the others and Max looked at Harper. "Let's give them a minute to get ready."

Max waited about sixty seconds then asked, "Everybody hear me? You got your earpieces on?"

"Yes, sir."

They listened another second then their boss's lips thinned and he drew in a breath. "That's everyone. Ian, what do you see with the garage?"

"No vehicles in sight. No people, either."

"All right. Are you ready?" he asked Harper.

"More than."

Max nodded and turned to lead the way. Riley settled back into the seat to watch and wait. He itched to be there with them, but it wasn't his place. Not this time. It might kill him, but he'd be patient and let them do their job.

Harper and Max approached the home with weapons ready. The dogs padded alongside them, noses twitching, ears alert to any command that might be uttered. Star alternated sniffing the ground and the air. King did the same. Max stopped at the front porch and Harper followed his lead. "Ian?"

"It's clear back here," he responded, his voice sounding like he was standing right next to her. "And the door is cracked. Looks like someone left in a hurry."

Max reached out a gloved hand and tried the door. "Front door is locked. Harper's coming around to back you up as you enter. I'll stay here in case someone decides to come out this way."

Harper and Star took off to the back of the house. She approached Ian and nodded.

"Entering the premises," he said and used a hand to push the door open slowly. Harper's adrenaline spiked, but she kept control over her breathing even while her pulse pounded. "Star, search."

"Careful." Max's voice came into her ear.

Ian held King back. Star would alert if there

was anyone there. Harper looked around the large open living area and found it to be nice and homey. A sofa against the wall. A coffee table and two end tables. Lamps on the end tables in their upright positions. The large area rug was clean and matched the quilted throw someone had thrown into the recliner opposite the fireplace. No sign of a struggle, no sign of anything other than that the occupants weren't there. "Clear in here."

Star headed down the hall, nose in the air, tail wagging. She returned a moment later and sat in front of Harper, tongue hanging from the side of her mouth. "Good girl, Star." Harper relaxed her defensive stance. "It's clear. There's no one in here."

Ian lowered his weapon and nodded to the kitchen. "Glasses on the counter."

Harper unlocked the front door and Max and Opal stepped inside. "Sit," Max told the dog. She sat. "Stay."

Harper walked over to look in the refrigerator. She pulled out a pack of ham. "Expires two weeks from now." She uncapped the milk and sniffed. "Still good."

"So someone *has* been living here. I'm going to check the closets."

He disappeared down the hall toward the bedrooms. Max placed his hands on his hips and pursed his lips. "All right, let's search the rest of this place and see what we can find."

Harper pulled the bag from her belt and opened it. Inside was a scarf that they'd taken from Penny's home for the dogs to use for tracking. She took it from the bag and held it out to Star. "Search, Star. Find Penny." Star sniffed the item then went to work once again.

"Search."

Star went straight to the wingback chair next to the fireplace and sat next to it. "She was here," Harper said. She praised the dog and offered her some food. Once Star devoured the treat, Harper encouraged her to search more. The canine covered every inch of the house, noting that Penny had been in each room. She then made her way to the sofa where she stopped and sniffed again. Then moved to the back of the couch and pawed at it. Harper pulled the cushions off.

Nothing.

"Max?"

"Yes?" He stood in the kitchen going through the rest of the items in the refrigerator.

"Help me move the couch, please?"

He headed over and together they moved the sofa away from the wall. Harper spotted what had gotten Star's attention. She picked up the cell phone with her gloved hand. "What do we have here?" She scratched the dog's ears. "Good girl, Star."

Max took the phone from her. "We'll get Dylan to work with this and see if he can trace it back to the owner."

"Could have been there awhile."

"True."

Harper pulled the packet of dog food from her pocket and gave Star some more. The dog ate it and then sat, ready to go to work again whenever Harper was ready.

Max tapped the screen. "Battery is low, but it's not dead. And it's not password-protected." He held it up and shook it slightly. "Between the food in the refrigerator and this, I'd say we missed Penny by a day or so."

"If not hours," Harper said. "We can send the phone off with the note that was left on my motel door earlier."

A knock on the door sounded and Riley poked his head in. "Is it all right if I come in?"

"Thought you promised to wait in the car."

He frowned. "I did, but Julianne said it was all clear and I could approach."

Harper shrugged. "The house is empty but they were here. Penny was anyway. The evidence shows we didn't miss them by much."

Max focused back on the phone. "Last number called was just two hours ago." He looked at Harper. "You nailed that one. We missed her by hours."

He dialed the number and put it on speaker. "Red Robin Inn, would you like to make a reservation?"

"Possibly," Max said. "Could you give me directions on how to find you?"

The man did so. Max thanked him and hung up. He looked at Harper, Ian and Riley. "I don't want to ask him anything about Penny or Jake over the phone, but that must be where she's headed. I don't want any possibility that he could tip them off. It's about thirty minutes from here. Let's get over there and see if she's checked in." He paused. "And don't everyone pull in the parking lot. Stay against the curb in the street. Harper…"

"Yes?"

"You talk to the guy at the front desk. I'll back you up. Ian, you and Julianne take the back of the building in case she somehow gets tipped off that we're coming." He frowned. "I'm tired of being one step behind. Let's go."

The team and their dogs once again piled back into the vehicle and caravanned it out onto the highway that would lead them to the motel. Harper eyed a stone-silent Riley in the passenger seat. "You okay?"

He glanced at her. "Sure. Why?"

"You seem quiet."

"Just thinking, I guess."

"About?"

"About my nephew and all he's been through over the past few months. I'm thinking how innocent people get caught up in things that can quickly spiral out of control through no fault of their own—and thinking that it's really not fair at all and that I hate feeling powerless to do anything about it. I really can't stand injustice."

She nodded. "I know. I see it all the time. Life definitely isn't fair, but we haven't been promised fair, just that we don't have to walk this journey alone."

"You're talking about God, I guess."

"I am."

"I'll admit, I've been pretty mad at Him for letting it all happen," he gritted out.

She shot him a glance then focused back on the road. "That's understandable."

"Maybe. You told me about your past, growing up with a dad who bailed on you and your mom. That had to have been hard."

"I'm sure it was. I don't remember much about it, to be honest. I just remember the fights stopped and that made me glad. It wasn't until I got older that I pieced together the whole story from relatives and my mom's drunken ramblings."

He gave her a contemplative look. "You ever get mad at God about it? Wonder why He didn't do something about it?"

"Sure, I've been there."

"But now?"

She shrugged. "I've made my peace with Him—and my past. In spite of my lousy upbringing, He's proved none of it took Him by surprise and now I can see how He's worked through the bad to bring good."

Riley fell silent again and Harper wished she could read his thoughts. "I don't think any good can come out of my sister's murder."

"I'm sure it looks that way now—and it may always look that way to you—us." She sighed. "I don't pretend to understand the ways or thoughts of God. I just know that *He* is good. He delights in us even in our imperfections and He despises evil." She cleared her throat. "And He's a just God. If I didn't believe that, I wouldn't do what I do. But murder is evil and you may never see any good in your sister's death."

"Seriously, what good could come of it?" he asked harshly.

She hesitated then lifted her shoulder in a slight shrug. "Maybe it's not a matter of looking for the good that can come from it, maybe it's more of just not letting Blackman win."

"And how do I do that?"

"As long as you and those who loved her become better people in spite of the pain that he's caused you by his evil actions, then he doesn't win. As long as you don't allow him to steal your joy and your love of life, then he doesn't win. If you go around hating him and being bitter the rest of your life, then essentially, he manages to kill you along with your sister." She released a breath. "You're not the same person now that you were before she died simply because what happened is a life-altering thing. But that difference doesn't have to define you or your future. You can still have a good life, Riley."

He swallowed hard but nodded for her to go on.

"Remember Charlotte and all she meant to you, teach Asher about her and keep her memory alive for him because he'll want to know more and more about her the older he gets. Don't let hating Blackman steal those moments that are sure to come."

Silence dropped between them. "I…never thought of it like that," he whispered. "I can't see past her death."

"It's only been a couple of months. It will take time. And when I said that good can actually come from bad," she said softly, "I suppose what I mean, in my case anyway, was that I chose to use that bad to bring good into the lives of others."

"Can you explain that?"

She drew in a deep breath. "I was faced with choices just like anyone else. Certain choices would bring good things. I could help others who were going through what I had already been through. I could give others hope that they could come out of their situation and be able to smile again, to be happy and…free." She sighed. "Or I could choose to go a different route and let anger and bitterness dictate my life. I didn't want to choose that route. But, because of what I've been through, I have a perspective that others don't have and I can help people in the same situations deal with their emotions and feelings in a constructive way."

"You became a better person in spite of your parents."

"Yes. That was a really rambling way of trying to make my point. I hope it made sense."

"It did." He fell silent yet again. Every so often she glanced at him, wondering what he was thinking. Her life hadn't been a bed of roses, for sure, but she was in a good place, proud of what she'd overcome and determined that she'd share her story with anyone she thought it could help.

She felt his gaze on her and glanced at him. "What?"

"You're different."

"What do you mean?"

He shrugged and let out a low laugh. "I'm not sure what I mean, to be honest. I just don't think I've ever met anyone like you."

"So is that a good thing?"

He smiled. "Yeah. It's a good thing."

Harper's insides twisted at his words. Why was he able to do that to her? Why did she have to meet him now when everything was in chaos? He needed to find Van and she needed to find Jake. Romance, attraction, dating… whatever. It was all a bad idea at this point in time and the thought saddened her more than she wanted to admit.

She concentrated on the driving and keeping her mouth shut. The more she opened it and shared with this man, the closer she grew to him. The more she talked, the more she invited him in to know the real her. Which kind of scared her.

Would he run away or stick around if he got to know her on a deeper-than-shallow-friendship level? Did she want to find out?

Yes.

No.

Maybe.

She wasn't going to answer that mental question right now. She was going to focus on her job.

The minutes passed and Harper finally pulled into the parking lot of the Red Robin Inn.

The others followed orders and parked on the street. She climbed from the vehicle and Riley did the same. Together they walked into the lobby of the motel with Star trotting at her side. "You don't get to go to the room, Riley."

"I know. I'll get back in the car when you tell me to."

Harper nodded and noted the motel smelled of cleaning solution and chlorine. To the right was the entrance to the indoor pool. To the left was the registration desk. A young man in his midtwenties chatted on the phone, his back to them.

Harper approached the desk and waited a moment. Then she slapped the old-fashioned bell sitting on the counter. The clerk jumped and spun. Then flushed. "I gotta go, Jess. Talk to you later." He hung up and cleared his throat. "Ah, sorry about that. What can I do for you?"

He seemed nice enough, just young.

You're not that much older, her inner voice mocked.

In reality, she might not be but a few years

older in numbers, but in life experience, chances were she was light-years away from this guy. She flashed her badge, which was overkill since the khaki pants and shirt with the FBI logo emblazoned on it stood out. Star sat at her side and waited for her orders. "I'm looking for a young woman by the name of Penny Potter. She would have been traveling with a little boy. A toddler."

The clerk, Jason, according to his nameplate, swallowed again and his eyes shifted to the door. "Ah, who? Oh, um, yeah, Ms. Potter. Let me check." He clicked a few keys on the computer while his eyes kept going toward the door then down to the phone.

"Something wrong?" Riley asked.

"What? Wrong?" He let out a nervous laugh. "No. Why?"

"Because you're awfully jumpy." Harper frowned. "Is Ms. Potter in your system or not?"

"Um. Yes. Yes, she is. She's right here. Yep. Here she is. She…ah…checked in about two hours ago. With a toddler." Another nerve-grating laugh.

What was wrong with this guy? "Give me her room number and a key, please," Harper said.

He flinched. "A key? And her room number? Why?"

"Because I asked for it. I'm working a case. You want to interfere with it?"

"Um. No. Of course not." With shaky fingers, he pulled a key from the stack and ran it through the machine. "There. 104. Just…um… around the corner."

Harper took the key. "Thanks."

Ian stepped inside. "Max sent me in to see if you needed any help."

Harper nodded at the clerk. "As a matter of fact, I need you to babysit for a few minutes. Make sure our friend here doesn't touch that phone until I give the all-clear, okay?"

"Sure thing." King settled himself beside Ian while Harper and Star readied themselves to head toward the room.

Harper drew in a deep breath. "Finally."

"What?" Riley asked. He walked beside her and stopped at the vehicle where he would wait.

"We're going to get some answers."

SIX

Riley sure hoped so. He was ready for this wild chase to be done with so he could get the money and head back to the hospital to be with Asher.

But until then…

He stayed back as ordered. It made his nerves itch to wait. He wanted to be in on the action, but while he was a former cop while living in Denver, until he earned a badge in this area, he'd have to hang back.

At least he had a good view of the room. He sat in the SUV with Max and Opal with the vehicle's windows down. Leo and True followed close behind Harper and Star. The other team members were poised for action as well, but would keep their distance until needed. Riley understood Max's desire for staunch caution. They didn't want to go bursting into the room without knowing where Penny and Kevin were—and where Jake might be with his gun.

Harper knocked on the door. "Housekeeping!"

No answer.

She tried again.

Again, nothing.

"Penny? You in there?"

She nodded at Leo. He nodded back. Harper swiped the key card and then they were in the room.

Riley realized he was holding his breath and forced himself to draw air into his lungs. For a moment all was quiet. Then Harper appeared in the doorway, her weapon lowered. "All clear," she called.

Max slammed a fist against the dash and Riley jumped then raised a brow. "Tense much?"

The man shot him a wry smile. "A little." Then he was out of the vehicle and joining the others.

Riley followed at a slower pace. Once at the room, he looked inside. Harper held the bag with Penny's scarf in her hand. Star continued to sniff the floor, the perfectly made beds, the chairs, the bathroom. Then she came to her handler and sat in front of her.

Harper let out a sigh. "She was never here." She swept a hand at the room. "I almost don't even need Star to tell me that. Look at this place. It's been cleaned and is ready for the next occupant."

"What?" Riley said. "I thought that guy said she checked in two hours ago."

"Obviously he lied. Or if she checked in, she never came to the room. I'm leaning toward him lying. Let's find out." Her nostrils flared and Riley was surprised he didn't actually see steam escape. She marched out of the room and down the sidewalk to the lobby. Riley stayed right behind her. No way was he missing this.

Harper strode past Ian and planted her hands on the chest-high counter. The young clerk gulped and took a step back. "Um...yes?"

"She was never in that room."

"Well...ah...why do you say that? Of course she was."

"Star says she wasn't. And my dog is never wrong. Which means you're lying and I want to know why."

He opened his mouth and she held up a hand. "Did she pay with credit card or cash?"

The man snapped his lips together.

Harper narrowed her eyes. "And before you answer, let me just help you out here. This is a federal investigation—one that is very important and is costing a lot of money. Now, you just sent us on a wild-goose chase. If you don't want to be arrested for obstructing justice, you'll tell me what you know and you won't leave out a single detail. Including the truth about whether or not Penny Potter and her son checked into that room."

The more she talked, the wider Jason's eyes grew. His Adam's apple bobbed continuously in his skinny throat while he listened to Harper's tirade. Finally, he held up his hands as though to ward her off. "I…I don't want any trouble."

"Good. Talk."

"A…um…a woman called a little while earlier and said if anyone came looking for her and a kid to tell them that she'd checked in. She said if I did, she'd give me a hundred bucks. I said okay. I didn't know it was the cops looking for her. I promise."

"You knew it when I walked in here."

He dropped his eyes to the counter and rubbed his chin. Then he gave a slight nod. "I did. I'm sorry. I wanted to help her—and I'll admit I could use the hundred dollars."

Harper's shoulders relaxed a fraction at his apology. Riley thought the guy certainly seemed sincere. "All right. Thanks for your… belated…help." She paused. "How was she going to get the hundred dollars to you?"

"She said she'd check in with me every once in a while."

"But she didn't give you a number?"

"No."

"And you really think she's going to check in with you so she can bring you a hundred bucks?"

Jason lowered his eyes and gave a small shrug. "It was worth a shot. And she called about thirty minutes before you got here to check."

Harper handed the young man a card. "If she calls again, you arrange to get your money, then you call me, you understand?"

"Um…sure."

"I mean it. I'm not kidding around here."

"No, ma'am. I believe you're not kidding around one bit. I'll call you if she calls me."

"Good. Now, I want the number she called from. Is it in your system?"

"Yes." At this point, he seemed eager to help. Probably wanted to do anything he had to in order to satisfy them and get them out of his hotel.

Harper wrote the number down and texted it to Dylan. She looked at Riley. "It's time to regroup, I would think. Let's check with Max and see where he wants to go from here."

Riley, impressed beyond measure and with a new respect for Harper and her ability to do her job, followed her out to join the rest of the waiting team who'd gathered in the parking lot. Before they reached them, he leaned over to whisper in her ear. "That was incredible."

"What?"

"You. Your interaction with him. That was some of the finest interrogating I've ever seen. And I've seen a lot."

A flush crept up into her cheeks and she gave a low laugh. "It was kind of fun, wasn't it? In the end. Initially, he just made me mad. I can't stand to be lied to. That kid gave off weird vibes from the moment we walked in. He better not try to lie on a regular basis, he's lousy at it."

"Which means he's most likely an honest person. Usually."

"I agree. Which made it a lot easier to get the truth out of him."

"Exactly. You would have made a great lawyer."

"Thank you, I'll pass on that one, though. I like my job." She gave small laugh. "Now let's see what Max has to say."

"Sure."

The team leader stepped forward. "All right everyone, let's head back to the motel. We can eat at the little restaurant there and develop a plan. The first thing we need to do is set up shifts. We can't all keep going twenty-four seven."

Harper's phone buzzed and she glanced at

it. "That's Dylan. He traced the number Penny called from and it was a throwaway phone."

"Of course it was," Max said. "She seems to have quite a supply of them, doesn't she?"

Harper nodded. "Let's get that food. I'm starving."

Harper stifled a yawn. She was feeling the effects of little sleep. But she also had adrenaline pumping through her. She settled Star in her spot in the vehicle while Riley took the passenger seat.

The drive back to the hotel passed mostly in silence as Riley kept his attention on the mirrors.

Setting up shifts sounded good to her. She needed some down time. Time to think and get her emotions under control when it came to Riley. Time to check her laptop to see if there were any updates on her father and time to decide what she really wanted from the future. She slid a glance at Riley and knew he was like the man she might *want* in her future, but was afraid to get too attached to the idea that it could possibly be him since it wasn't likely to pan out anyway. But someone like him...yeah, that wouldn't be so bad.

She couldn't help smiling at the thought of being a lawyer, though. Truthfully, the idea didn't bother her nearly as much as it probably should. As a lawyer, she wouldn't be traveling as much. She could stay home with any future children she and her husband might have.

Harper sucked in a breath and put the brakes on that line of thinking. A husband and children were not in her immediate future.

Her phone buzzed and she pressed the button that would send the call to her Bluetooth. "Harper here."

"It's Dylan again."

"Back so soon? That's got to be good. What's up?"

"I checked out that Van Blackman character. He's definitely not one of the good guys."

"I have no doubt about that. Do you have any way of finding him?"

She felt Riley's gaze on her. "No, he seems to have dropped off the grid. If you have a number for him, I might be able to find something through that."

"Let me ask." She looked at Riley. "Do you have a cell number for Blackman?"

He shook his head. "He's using disposable phones. Whatever number I had for him is no longer in service."

"Did you get that, Dylan?" she asked.

"I got it. He's got a credit card he used a

couple of weeks ago. It was a large cash advance from one of the banks in Drum Creek so it's definitely possible he's still in the area. I'll keep a watch on the card and let you know if he uses it again."

"Thanks, Dylan." She pulled into the parking lot of the motel, said goodbye to their tech guy and climbed out of the vehicle with Star at her side.

The team gathered in the dining area once again, drawing the stares of everyone already there. Harper noticed and simply acknowledged them with a nod and a smile. So much for staying under the radar. When all six of them were together, it really wasn't possible to be inconspicuous.

A young boy about the age of seven approached and held out a hand. "Can I pet him?"

She smiled. "Sure. But it's very good that you asked first. And Star is a girl."

He grinned and a deep dimple flashed in one cheek. "She's pretty—and *big*." Star relished the child's sweet touch. Harper found Riley watching the pair, longing and despair mingled in his eyes. She could clearly see that he was thinking of his nephew and her heart hurt for him. When the little boy's mother pulled him away from Star, Harper reached for Riley's hand and squeezed it. He smiled his thanks. A sad smile that disappeared when his jaw tightened with determination.

Max's phone rang and he stepped away to answer while the others discussed the next step in the case. When he returned, he cleared his throat. "Riley, could you excuse us for a moment?"

Riley's gaze shifted back and forth between Max and Harper then he shrugged and stepped out of hearing distance.

"What is it?" Harper asked.

"That was one of the US marshals we're working with. Thomas Grant. Esme Dupree called him."

Harper scratched Star's ears. "She did?"

"Yeah."

Esme Dupree was their star witness in hiding. She had seen her brother, Reginald Dupree, murder someone he worked with. Reginald knew that she'd seen him and was out to make sure she didn't testify against him. By agreeing to testify, Esme had put herself in grave danger.

"Did she say where she was hiding out?" Harper asked. Esme had been in the Witness Protection Program, but after a close call, had ditched the marshals and struck out on her own.

Max sighed. "No, just that she's alive and still planning to testify at the trial."

"But she still refuses to come in?" Ian prodded.

"Yes." Max rubbed his head then shook it.

"We need her testimony to put him away," Harper said impatiently. "Without her, we have no case."

"Well, I can't say I blame her for being a little wary. Being told you were safe and then getting found and almost killed would make anyone doubt the marshal's abilities."

"Not to mention the fact that two women who resembled her were killed."

"Yeah," Ian grunted. "That would have done it for me, for sure."

Max shook his head. "Thomas tried to convince her to come in, but she says she doesn't trust anyone at this point."

"Anything else?" Ian asked.

"The number she was calling from was traced back to a disposable phone," Max said.

"Esme wouldn't call if she thought they'd be able to find her," Harper reminded them. "She's not stupid."

"Except for running away from the program thinking she can take care of herself better than the US Marshals can," Ian said. "That's stupid in my book."

"I don't know," Harper said. "It might be why she's still alive."

Ian frowned at her. "You think someone on the inside is a mole?"

"I don't know that either, but she was found when she shouldn't have been found. The Marshals have a sterling track record. So it does make one wonder."

Max fell silent. They all did while they contemplated her words.

Harper caught Riley's eye from afar and nodded. He approached them as his phone buzzed. "Sorry," he muttered. He glanced at the screen then answered. "Hey, Champ. How are you doing?" A pause. "Of course you can call me. You can call me anytime."

Harper didn't mean to eavesdrop, but Riley didn't seem to require privacy. "A clown came to visit, huh?… Yeah?… And you thought it was me?" He chuckled even as a flash of pain darkened his eyes. "I'll be by to see you soon, kiddo, I promise."

Asher must have said something else because Riley scowled. "No, I haven't caught him yet, but I'm closing in on him… Yeah?…I wish you could help catch him, too, but you just concentrate on getting better, okay?… Okay, then." Another pause. "Yes, I'm still thinking about the puppy you want… Uh-huh… Okay. Love you, Champ."

He listened a moment longer then hung up, jaw working, eyes glittering with suppressed rage.

The team members had grown quiet, listening to the conversation. Harper caught his arm. "He asked you if you'd caught Blackman, didn't he?"

"Yeah. I didn't realize he knew as much..." He drew in a deep breath. "But yes, he asked and said he wanted to help."

"I gathered that."

Riley's fingers curled into fists. "I have to get him, Harper," he said hoarsely.

"I know. I understand." And she did. She might not understand *exactly* how he felt due to the fact she'd never had a sibling killed by someone who was supposed to love her, but she understood the determination to not let someone get away with doing wrong. Jake Morrow had been a trusted member of the unit, a man they'd treated as one of them, someone she would have trusted with her life and even died for.

Now, he was a wanted man. And Harper desperately wanted to find him so she could demand answers from him. She could see that going over well. Arrogant and cocky, Jake wouldn't respond well to demands. He liked to do the demanding. But he'd been an excellent agent and part of the team and, because of that, he deserved a chance to explain himself.

"Van's taunting me," Riley bit out. "Following me then disappearing as though to say, 'You might get close, but you won't catch me.'"

"He'll mess up sooner or later and when he does, you'll be there to grab him. Or we will."

He gave her a faint smile. "Thanks."

Max rubbed a hand over his head. "All right. To recap. Penny's on the run. It looks like Jake's after her. We've got law enforcement cooperation and Dylan's keeping tabs on his cell phone."

"Which he's not going to use if he doesn't want to be found," Ian muttered.

"And it's looking more and more like he doesn't want to be," Max agreed. "But I want to know why."

Riley's phone buzzed again. He glanced at the screen and frowned. "Let me take this."

"Of course."

This time he stepped away from the group and pressed the phone to his ear.

"Man, that sounds like some tough stuff he's dealing with," Max said in a quiet voice. "What's wrong with his nephew?"

"He was shot when his mother's boyfriend opened fire on them at a grocery store. He killed the mother, Riley's sister, and paralyzed Asher. The poor kid has a bullet lodged near his spine. That's why Riley's so determined to bring in Jake. He needs the money for Asher's surgery to help him walk again."

Max let out a low whistle.

"What if we could help?" Ian said.

Harper lifted a brow. "Help how?"

Ian shrugged. "Why don't I call Dylan and see what we can come up with?"

"I'm on the way," Riley said as he headed toward the front door.

Harper caught up to him. "Everything okay? Is Asher all right?"

"That wasn't about Asher. That was a friend of mine who works at the grocery store up the street. He said Van Blackman was just in there buying some ibuprofen and cold medicine." He took off and Harper rose to go after him then paused to look over her shoulder. "Max?"

"Go," he said. "Watch his back."

"Thanks. Star, heel." The dog bolted to her side and they hurried after a disappearing Riley. She caught up to him crossing the street. "Riley."

He shot her a tight look then entered the store. An older gentleman approached and pointed out the door. "He just left not five minutes ago."

"Which way did he go?"

"North."

Riley turned to look. "Back toward the park," he murmured. "What's he driving?"

"A green Ford pickup."

"We can take my vehicle if you want," Harper said.

He nodded. "I have to try to find him."

"Let's go. We'll call Max and let him know what's going on."

They rushed back to the hotel parking lot where they climbed into her vehicle. Star hopped into her spot and soon Harper was headed down the road in the direction of the park.

Park made it sound small. Searchable. But as Harper had discovered, it was a vast area of acreage with a multitude of hiding places. However, Riley had done the smart thing and asked people to keep an eye out for the man he was hunting. If Blackman was camping out in the park, then he'd have to come into town for supplies every so often—and to search for Riley, apparently.

Whatever the case, it had paid off. Once again someone had spotted him and called it in.

They just had to catch up to him now.

Riley gripped the door handle as Harper took the next turn. The green truck was just ahead but getting ready to disappear around the next curve. He wanted to tell her to hurry, go faster, but he knew she was doing her best to keep them far enough behind so the man ahead wouldn't know they were on his tail. And besides, she could only go so fast on the winding, two-lane road.

They were climbing now, the road slanting upward, the drop-off to Harper's left growing steeper. "Come on," he whispered.

Harper spared him a glance before turning her attention back to the road. Riley hadn't realized he'd spoken aloud.

The green truck disappeared for another moment. Approximately twenty seconds later, when Harper took the next curve, a flash of green to his right caught his eye. "Watch out!" He realized what was going to happen in the split second before the front of the green truck slammed into the passenger door. He jerked against the seat belt then was tossed back against the window.

Harper cried out. The wheel spun out of her hands and the SUV skidded along the edge of the road. The green pickup came again and this time the nudge was almost gentle in comparison. Through the windshield Riley met Van's wild gaze and his gleeful, crazed expression as the man didn't back away, but continued to accelerate and push the big SUV toward the side of the cliff. "Hang on, Harper, we're going over!"

Harper pressed the gas, and the SUV lunged forward, but it was too late.

The big green pickup's engine gave a mighty roar, another surge forward and the SUV went off the road and over the side of the embankment.

Star barked then yelped when the SUV turned onto its driver's side and bumped down the steep cliff. The seat belt kept Riley in his seat, his right hand gripping the handle while he braced himself for impact. Trees flew past, dirt and rocks pinged off the windows, the world tilted and jounced them and he thought he might be sick.

Then came the bone-jarring halt. The slam jerked him hard enough for him to lose his grip on the door handle. And then all was still. For a moment he didn't move, his breathing—and body—suspended, held physically in place by the seat belt. His heart thundered in his ears.

Finally, he was able to catch his breath. "Harper?" He looked over to find her crammed against the driver's door. Her eyes were open, but glazed. "Harper! You okay?"

She blinked. Then blinked again. "Yes. I think so. You?"

"Yeah. Did you hit your head?"

"No. Surprisingly. And I think my vest protected me from having much of a bruise from my seat belt." She grunted and turned, trying to see behind her. "Star? Star!"

A low woof came from the back and he saw her eyes close in relief for a fraction of a second.

"I'm pretty stuck. Can you get out?" she asked.

"I'm not sure. If I unhook my seat belt, I'm going to fall into you."

Her hand patted her hip. "My phone's gone. Must have popped off." She reached for the dangling mic of the radio while Riley searched for his phone. He heard her calling to her coworkers and getting no response. She let go of the mic in disgust. "It's dead."

His fingers closed over the phone that had wedged between the center console and the seat. "What's the number?"

She gave it to him and Max answered on the first ring. "Max, this is Riley. We got ambushed and could use a little help."

"What's wrong?" the man barked. "Where are you?"

Riley told him as best he could. "Just follow the road and keep looking down. You'll see us." He looked up through the passenger window.

"We didn't fall too far. I can see the edge of the road. Maybe about twenty feet?"

"We're on the way. Stay on the phone, we'll track it and make things a lot easier."

"Of course." He should have just suggested that.

A loud crack reached him and the back windshield shattered. Riley hollered and he heard Harper give a startled cry. "He's shooting at us!"

"What's going on?" Max hollered.

Another bullet rocked the vehicle and Riley dropped the phone. Max would have to figure it out for himself. Riley grabbed for the door handle and unbuckled his seat belt. Gravity pulled him toward her and while he did his best not to land fully on top of her with his entire weight, she still gave a grunt when his elbow dug into her side.

Bracing himself on the back of the seat, he climbed into the back so that he was standing on the shattered rear door window. Star lay above him in her secure area, her paws slipping through the barred door. "Come on, Harper, we're sitting ducks. We've got to get out of here." He reached around to release her belt and found she was already moving. "We'll have to go out the back."

"The back that he's shooting at?"

"Afraid so."

Two more bullets pinged off the undercarriage. She flinched, but lifted her chin. "He's moved. Those bullets came from a different direction."

"Yeah. I've got Star. I don't want her walking and cutting her feet on the glass near here." Riley released Star from her cage and caught her in his arms. She wiggled, but he held her tight.

"Star, stay."

The dog flattened her ears, but immediately went still at Harper's command.

Another bullet, then a rapid succession of them battered the bottom of the SUV.

Harper gripped his bicep. "He's aiming for the gas tank. Go!"

SEVEN

Harper's head beat a harsh rhythm in her skull as Riley awkwardly scrambled over into the back with Star still in his arms. She pressed a hand to her temple. She didn't remember hitting her head in the tumble down the side of the cliff.

She figured it was just the rush of adrenaline, combined with her erratic pulse that caused it to pound like a jackhammer. She drew in several deep breaths while she fought her way to the back of the vehicle. Riley stayed at the very edge of the back. All he had to do was step out. She moved close to him. "Ready?"

"Ready when you are."

Star whined in Riley's arms, but continued to let him hold her as long as she could see Harper.

She drew in a steadying breath then nodded. Riley pushed Star out the back and clambered behind her. He turned and reached for Harper's hand and she grasped his fingers to let him help her out.

Sirens sounded from up above, but Harper's quick rush of relief didn't last long as the crack of more gunshots split the air. Bullets pelted the ground and the SUV and Harper expected to feel the slam of one at any second. Or hear the explosion. "Go!"

Together they raced for the trees. Two more pops sounded and a bullet caught her in the upper back. She cried out and went down.

"Harper!"

Pain streaked through her. She couldn't breathe, couldn't move, couldn't speak. Her hands clawed the ground, her lungs strained for air.

"Harper!" He dropped beside her. Star barked. The sound of the engine roaring away echoed through her head. "Let me see. Don't move."

Not moving was not going to be a problem. Finally, a breath caught and she pulled it in eagerly. Then coughed. The sirens screamed louder. She dragged in another desperate breath and grimaced. "He's getting away," she rasped.

"He's just going to have to this time," Riley said. "He shot you."

Harper drew in another breath. "He shot… my vest. Just…knocked the wind…out of me."

Riley raked a shaky hand through his hair and Star padded over to nudge Harper's cheek. She scratched the animal's ear. "Good girl."

Star sat beside her with a woof. Harper continued to concentrate on breathing through the fire shooting through her, waiting for it to ebb. Riley stayed beside her, watching, his weapon ready. She appreciated his vigilance.

"Harper? Riley?"

Max's anxious shout made Harper grimace. She gripped Riley's hand. "Help me sit up." He hesitated and she sighed. "I'm getting up with or without your help. *With* would simply make it easier." She looked up. "Down here, Max!"

Riley's jaw tightened and he pulled her into a sitting position. Fire blazed through her back and stars danced before her eyes, but she'd heard stories from others who'd been shot and hit in the vest so knew the feeling was normal. She'd be fine. Bruised and sore, but fine. Eventually.

But that was okay. It was better than being dead.

Max's head appeared over the drop-off. "You okay?"

"Yes. Need a BOLO for a green truck." She drew in another breath then gave him the license number. Wow. It hurt to yell, too.

"On it. Can you climb up or do we need to come get you?"

"We can climb, I think." She muttered the last two words under her breath and saw that Riley heard them. He lifted a brow. "Let's go," she said before he could suggest they let someone come get them. "It's not that far."

"I'm not going to talk you out of trying, am I?" Riley asked.

"Probably not. Ask me again in a couple of minutes."

"All right then, I'm game if you are."

Together, with Star at her side, they made their way up the dirt hill. Some places were easier to navigate than others, but the drop-off hadn't been straight down, more like a gentle slope. Which was what had saved their lives.

That and the tree.

She didn't want to think about it. She knew the area had some really steep and deadly inclines, and that if one fell—or was run off the road—it could be fatal. Once back up on the road, Max, Ian and Zeke rushed over. A chopper roared overhead and Harper looked up. "We've got him looking for the truck," Max explained.

"Come on," Riley said, "let's have a look at your back." Harper let him help her off with the vest. She hissed as she moved her shoulder.

Ian stared at her with concern. "You got hit?"

"Yes. Well, the vest did. I'm okay."

She rotated her shoulder and breathed a sigh of relief that nothing felt broken. It hurt like crazy, and was bruised for sure, but it was nothing that would keep her from working.

Max stopped her. "Let me check it."

"It should be all right in time. It's just a bruise."

"Do you mind if I take a look anyway?"

"Of course not."

Harper waited while Max felt the area and in spite of her gasp and groan, he pronounced her correct in her own assessment. "Wouldn't hurt to have it x-rayed to make sure there isn't something small like a fracture, but I won't force it if you say you're good."

She hesitated. "If it's not better in a couple of days, I'll go in."

"You feel up to working?"

"Yes. I'm up to it."

Max nodded. "Good enough, then."

Star sat by her, panting. "Can one of you give her some water?"

"Sure." Ian jogged to his vehicle and grabbed some from the back, along with a bowl. And two more bottles that he handed to Harper and Riley.

Satisfied that Star was fine, Harper could

focus on the incident. She took a long swig from the bottle then recapped it. "That was Blackman in that truck. He's quite determined to kill Riley."

"And you along with him, apparently," Max said darkly.

"No, he's not one to worry overmuch about collateral damage," Riley said.

"Well, killing either of us isn't an option." Harper set her jaw and narrowed her eyes. "We just have one more fugitive to catch in addition to Jake."

Max nodded. "All right. We've got the BOLO out on both of them now. I'm not sure why, but neither one seems to be in a hurry to leave this area."

"Well, we know why Jake is still here. It means he believes Penny is close by."

"And Van knows I'll track him wherever he goes," Riley said. "The thing is he's got a good setup here." He rubbed his head. "He's got everything he needs. Water, food and any number of hiding places. I'm pretty sure that's why he's still here. He grew up in this area and knows it like the back of his hand."

"Where's his family now?" Max asked.

"They live near here in Estes Park."

"Have you talked to them?"

Riley nodded. "The detectives talked to

them the day she was shot, of course. Then first thing after Charlotte's funeral, I went by to see them." He exhaled a quick breath. "I believe I told you before that he grew up in foster homes. But his family is located here. A scattering of them anyway. They're still in trouble with the law and don't have much use for law enforcement, but his mother seemed pretty horrified when I told her what had happened and cried the whole time I was there. She claimed she hadn't heard from Van in years."

"And yet he stayed in the area."

He nodded. "I wasn't so sure I bought her story so I had several former cop buddies of mine take turns sitting on his home, but he never showed. Either she really did refuse to have anything to with him or he's just smart and figured there would be someone watching to see if he showed up. In any event, he hasn't gone by there since. At least as far as I know. I check in with his mother pretty regularly and I have some buddies that make their presence visible a few times a week."

"So what would keep him here? Why not run as far and as fast as he could?"

Riley shrugged. "No idea. If it's not his mother, it's very possible there was some connection with his dead wife's family. Van and his wife, Susie, met in foster care. She came from an abusive situation as well. The way he talked, it sounded like their similar backgrounds bonded them. And that's about all he would say about his past." He scrubbed a hand across his jaw. "I talked to his last foster mother just a few weeks ago and she just said he wasn't any trouble even as a teenager, but she still wouldn't trust him as far as she could throw him. Said he was just too quiet and introverted and she never knew what he was thinking."

"What happened to his wife? Did he kill her, too?" Harper asked.

"No. She died in childbirth."

"Oh. That's sad."

"Like I said, he refused to talk much about it. Just that he'd been married once. Charlotte told me a little bit about him and I looked up the rest."

"All right, then." Max nodded. "Let's hope someone spots them and calls it in."

Riley's eyes turned toward the national park. "I think it's time for an all-out search of that area. We'll have to do it mostly on foot, though. There are places vehicles can't go. What do you think?"

Harper looked at Max who shrugged. "It's better than anything else we've got right now."

Riley nodded. "The sun's going to be setting soon. First thing in the morning would be a good time to get started."

"If we don't get any tips or anything else before morning, that'll be the plan."

"Works for me," Ian said.

Zeke blew out a breath. "Yeah. Works for me, too."

"What about the chopper?" Harper asked. "Do we need to bring it in?"

"Might not be a bad idea," Max said. "I'll them know."

Zeke ran a hand through his hair and shook his head.

"We'll find him, Zeke," Harper reassured him.

"I know. The question is, who will we find? Simply a rogue agent who needs some serious redirection or a lousy traitor?"

Either one didn't sound good. And Harper knew which one she was leaning toward.

Traitor.

Even thinking the word made her sick to her stomach. She grimaced and prayed no one else would get hurt before they could find Van and Jake.

Sitting in the back of Ian's SUV with King and Star beside him, Riley had to admit he was worried. Worried about his nephew, worried about putting Harper in the crosshairs of a killer. And worried that if she—or someone else—died at Van's hand, it would be Riley's fault.

On the way back to the motel, he called his mother to check in on her.

"No change," she murmured. "He misses his mama."

Tears cloaked her words and Riley shut his eyes against the surge of hate that wanted to take over. He couldn't let it. It would cloud his thinking, make him careless. For now, he had to bury it. "I know. I miss her, too."

"We all do."

He paused. "What should I do, Mom?" he rasped.

"What do you mean?"

He swallowed hard then forced the words from his throat. "Should I quit chasing Blackman? Should I come back and stay with Asher? What would be the best thing to do? The best thing for Asher?" His heart had never felt so torn. He wanted justice for his sister. He wanted Van Blackman behind bars. Or dead. And yet he didn't want it at the expense of his nephew's mental and emotional well-being. Asher came first.

"Asher will be fine," his mother finally said after a lengthy silence. "He sleeps a lot because of the pain medicine. And while he asks about you every day, I think you need to stay after Van. Catch him and put him away so he can't do this to another family."

Riley's heart squeezed with grief and anger. "Right." It was what he'd hoped she'd say and yet, part of him had wanted her permission to quit so he could be there for Asher.

He drew in a deep breath and pictured his sister's pretty face. Smiling, laughing, spinning in circles with the son she'd adored. His resolve hardened. His mother was right. He couldn't let the man move on to find another woman to kill—another family to devastate. And Riley knew with everything in him that Van would do so the minute he thought he was free to pursue another woman without watching over his shoulder for Riley to show up and take him in. "Okay, Mom, give him a hug for me and tell him I love him."

"You know I will." She paused. "And son, please be careful. I can't lose you, too. I…I don't think I'd survive it."

His heart hurt at her words. "I'll be careful, Mom."

He hung up and dropped his chin to his chest while his mind raced. Okay, so, in the morning, they'd start hunting again. *God, if You're listening, we could use some divine intervention here. Please?*

A rap on the window snagged his attention. He opened the door to Harper's lovely face and clouded eyes. "Are you all right?" she asked.

"I should be asking you that question. You're the one who got shot."

She offered him a faint smile and some of the clouds receded. "I'm still breathing, so I'm grateful and count that as having a good day."

"I know the feeling. So, what's the plan?"

"They're finishing up here, gathering what evidence they can to ship back to Montana for the lab to go over."

"But this doesn't have anything to do with your case."

She smiled again. "But Max agreed to let you have every resource at your disposal for your help in finding Jake. Our state-of-the-art lab is one of those resources."

He nodded. "I appreciate that. Although, I feel like I've got the better end of the deal. We haven't seen or heard anything more about Morrow."

"That's not your fault. We know he was here. We know Penny was here, could possibly still be here. As long as she stays in the area, Morrow will, too, and we'll find him eventually. So," she said, "it looks like you're going to need an extra set of eyes. Now that we know the lengths Blackman will go to get rid of you, we plan to watch out for you and make sure he doesn't have another chance to get at you."

Riley was grateful for the help. He'd been fighting his own emotions for so long, his search for Van a mostly solitary endeavor, that the thought of having backup was a huge relief. "I don't see how you can prevent it, but I sure won't turn down the offer of the resources—and the extra set of eyes."

"Perfect. I guess we can head back to the motel. The tow truck will be here soon."

"What are you going to do for a vehicle?"

She studied him. "What do you drive again?"

He laughed and shook his head as he realized she'd driven them everywhere they'd gone together. He found he didn't mind that at all. Harper was strong, capable—and extremely attractive. "I have a blue pickup with a king cab."

"That'll work."

Riley watched her walk toward one of the other Suburbans and let out a half chuckle. Then sobered. "Wait a minute," he called. "Are you serious?"

EIGHT

Harper was serious. Until another vehicle could be delivered, they would have to improvise. She looked at Riley and smiled. "I would appreciate it, of course, but you don't have to if you don't want to. I'm not twisting your arm."

"But?"

"But it would help us keep the investigation going at full speed if we don't have to worry about someone being left without a ride for the next day or so. We can always rent what we need, but that means heading to the nearest airport or waiting to have something delivered—and then it won't be equipped with everything we might need for a search out here in the middle of nowhere. If we use your truck, I can just transfer the stuff from mine to yours."

His lip quirked into a half grin. "I get it. You don't have to do any arm-twisting. I'll share."

"Thanks."

Once they were finished with the scene, she, Star and Riley climbed into Max's vehicle.

Since half of the backseat was taken up with Opal's area, Harper directed the canine to the very rear. Harper let Riley have the front passenger seat and she settled in next to Opal. Max cranked the Suburban and they headed out.

"All right, let's talk about Jake for a minute. What are we missing?" Harper asked.

Her boss shook his head. "I'm not sure. I think our best course of action is to stick to the plan. We'll pull in the chopper and do a full-on search of the park area tomorrow like we planned. For now, though, let's get some food."

"You don't think the chopper will be too much of a neon sign, saying, 'Hey, we're here and looking for you'?" Riley asked wryly.

Max shook his head. "They know we're here. Maybe if we keep their attention on the sky, they won't see us coming from the ground."

Riley nodded and shrugged. "Works for me."

"All right. We'll start first thing in the morning."

A quick stop at one of the local fast-food places filled their bellies and a short time later Max pulled into the motel parking lot followed by the other four agents. She appreciated their concern and their willingness to rush to the rescue. She worked with good people.

As far as she knew.

Jake was one she just wasn't sure about.

Harper knew one thing. She was tired. She loved her job, no doubt about it, but it was demanding and high stress and she'd admit she was ready to unwind for a little while. Maybe watch some television with Star curled up at her feet.

And Riley at her side.

She blinked. Now where did *that* come from?

She huffed. She might as well admit it. She found him attractive. There. She said it. Well, thought it anyway. But it didn't matter. There was no way she was getting involved with him.

Then again, why not?

Because he hadn't come out and said he was interested? Okay, there was that, but she had a feeling he was.

Then there was the small fact that he lived ten hours away from her.

She thought about her small one-bedroom condo back in Billings, Montana. White walls, a few pictures of her and the team and Star, of course. But mostly stark and blank, it was simply a place to sleep and shower. Longing crashed in on her, threatening to smother her. She wanted more than that. She wanted a home, a family, a place and person to call her own.

Harper drew in a deep breath and pushed

aside the feelings. She had a case to solve. Dreams were nice to have if they were one day attainable. Harper wasn't sure hers were. She wasn't even sure she knew how to have a relationship at this point. Her parents hadn't exactly been domestic role models. Although, at least she knew what she *didn't* want in a marriage.

"Harper?"

She blinked. Riley stood in front of her, Star had joined her at her side. And she didn't even remember climbing from the vehicle. She cleared her throat. "Sorry, I was thinking."

"Deeply. You okay?"

"Sure. I'm fine." She looked behind him to see Max studying her, a frown on his face. "I'll see you guys in the morning."

She headed to her room, her heart in conflict. She could have died tonight. But she'd come close to death several times so what made this time different?

The fact that Riley was with her and he could have died, too?

Maybe.

Inside her room, Star settled herself on the bed and Harper removed her gear. She checked her weapon and made sure the safety was on, then unstrapped the knife at her ankle and set it on the end table along with her phone and little black notepad.

As soon as she flopped onto the bed next to Star, her phone buzzed. She groaned and rolled to snag it.

Riley.

Harper sat up. "Hello?"

"I know you're tired and if you'd rather just sleep, I understand, but you want to get a cup of coffee in the lobby?"

"As long as it's decaf."

"I'm ready when you are."

"Give me five."

Harper hung up and swung her legs over the side of the bed. All of a sudden, she wasn't tired at all. She chuckled to herself. If the thought of spending time with Riley could banish her fatigue after a long, tumultuous day, she needed to take him with her on *all* of her assignments.

She ran her fingers through her hair and noticed it had grown quite a bit. When was the last time she'd taken time to have it cut? Harper wondered if Riley preferred long hair or short.

She huffed at her thoughts. What did it matter? They could be friends, nothing more. She wasn't going to do a long-distance relationship assuming Riley was even interested.

So why was she running gloss over her lips?

Ugh. Harper tossed the tube back into her toiletries bag and zipped it.

She donned a light jacket with a side pocket

and slipped her weapon inside then checked outside her room using the window and the peephole. Riley stood to the side waiting on her. Harper opened the door and stepped out. Her heart thudded an extra beat at the sight of him. He'd dressed in sweat pants and a dark blue T-shirt that brought out his tan—and stretched nicely over his shoulder muscles. She cleared her throat and realized she was going to have to come to terms with the fact that she was drawn to this man. And not just because he was good-looking, but because she liked him. A lot.

Riley smiled. "That was fast."

"I've learned how to get ready to walk out the door in under a minute. You shouldn't be waiting out here in the open."

"I was only here a few seconds before you opened the door."

"Doesn't take long to pull the trigger once you're in the sights."

"Noted."

They started walking. He stepped around her and she instantly noticed the protective gesture. Harper cut her eyes to him. "I'm not the one he wants to kill," she said softly.

He shrugged and kept walking. "Maybe not, but he won't mind going through you to get to me. I'm going to do my best to make sure that doesn't happen."

Her own protective instincts surged, but she squelched them. Riley was old-fashioned enough to respond to his natural instincts when it came to women and danger. And yet he wasn't offensive about it or thought she couldn't take care of herself, he just wanted to do it.

Frankly, Harper was surprised she'd picked up on that aspect of his personality so quickly. And actually liked it. She was always taking care of other people. It might be nice to be taken care of for once.

He opened the door and held it while she stepped inside the lobby. "The problem is," he said, "I can take all the precautions in the world, but eventually, you and I both know that if Blackman wants me dead, if I don't get him first, he'll get me."

"Let's make sure we get him first, then."

They went to the coffee urns and helped themselves. Harper and Star took a seat in the far corner with Harper placing her back to the wall and her front toward the door. It was a habit she knew she'd probably never break.

Riley maneuvered a chair so he could sit next to her. Apparently it was his habit, too. She took a sip of the hot brew and smiled into the cup before looking up. "How's Asher doing?"

"Hanging in there."

"And your mother?"

"The same." He frowned. "I could hear the fatigue in her voice when I called tonight. She rarely goes home and it's taking a toll on her."

"She won't let anyone else sit with Asher?"

He shrugged. "Every once in a while. The ladies in her Bible study group are wonderful. They offer, but she says it's just easier to stay than to worry from a distance. If I were there, she would go home more, I'm sure."

"You're questioning whether you should continue the search or go to Asher."

He raised a brow. "I am." He shrugged. "In fact, I discussed that with Mom again tonight. She promised to let me know if it gets to be too much for her, but I doubt she will."

"I'm sorry you're having to go through all of this."

He drew in a deep breath and let it out slowly. "I am, too. But once Van is behind bars and Asher has had his surgery, it'll all be uphill from there." He sipped his coffee and stared at the front door and Harper figured his mind was on his nephew.

He blinked and shook his head.

She covered his hand with hers. When he looked up, she said, "Tell me about your sister. What was she like?"

A glow entered his eyes. "She was an amazing big sister and a natural mother. She was three years older than I and, trust me, she practiced her mothering skills on me when we were younger. She liked black licorice and coke when she watched a movie." He grimaced. "I never could stand that stuff. The licorice, I mean. She had a heart for the less fortunate and often volunteered on holidays to feed the homeless."

"What about Asher's father?"

Riley cleared his throat. "Bryce McDowell. He was a good guy. He and Charlotte were high school sweethearts and got married right after graduation, but couldn't figure out what he wanted to do with his life so he joined the military. He wound up serving in the Middle East. Before he left, she got pregnant with Asher, and then he was killed about two months after he was there."

"Oh, how awful for her."

"Yes. Asher never knew his father. Then when Asher was three, Charlotte met Van Blackman. He wooed her and she thought he was the best thing. We all did. One afternoon, about two years after they were together and talking marriage, I came out of a restaurant and saw him coming out of a hotel across the street at the same time. I started to call out to him when a pretty blonde walked up and kissed him." He glanced at her. "And trust me, it wasn't a sisterly kiss."

She grimaced.

"Anyway, I confronted him and he tried to lie his way out of it. I refused to believe him and he took a swing at me."

"How did that work out for him?"

A grim smile pulled his lips flat. "I ducked. He didn't. I told my sister what I saw and she asked him to explain himself. He admitted the woman was a former girlfriend and had asked him to meet her. He did, but said he immediately regretted it and begged her forgiveness. She told him she wanted some time to think about it."

"And he started stalking her?"

"Yes, but she didn't mention it until it was really too late for me to do anything about it. He killed her the next week after I'd started the process to procure a restraining order." He rubbed his eyes. "Some days I wish I'd never said anything."

"Could you really not have told her?"

He shook his head. "No. I had to tell her, I just wish I'd been more careful, more watchful—more aware. I was a cop and I missed it. Completely. It's hard to forgive myself for that."

"She never told you he was stalking her?"

"No. And I'm not sure it occurred to her to label it stalking. She'd mention seeing him in strange places. He'd show up at her job, at her church, at the same restaurant if she was out with friends, but she never said he was stalking her. In hindsight, that's what it was, of course." He cleared his throat and looked away. She let the silence fill the space between them.

He finally looked back at her. "What about you? You told me about your parents and a little about what your childhood was like. Do you have any other family?"

"I have a few aunts and uncles that I never see. They were around some when I was younger, but not anymore. I suppose that's why I want to have a big family one day."

"How big?"

"I don't know. Several kids, I guess. I want the proverbial white picket fence, too." She laughed then sighed. "Maybe I'm asking for too much. I want a guy who's crazy about me, kids and dogs." She shrugged. "One day."

"So you want to quit the Bureau?"

She frowned and pursed her lips then shook her head. "No, not really. I love what I do. It's been my life for a long time now so I'm not sure I could quit even if I wanted to, but I wouldn't mind the option."

"I see."

Riley stiffened. Her words threw his guard up. What was he doing talking about the future? Or even thinking about it? He had a murderer to catch and a nephew to care for. He didn't have time for romance. No matter that the attraction and temptation to get to know her better was strong.

Why her?

"What is it?" she asked.

"What do you mean?"

"You just got all quiet. What are you thinking?"

"A lot of things. Mostly that I wish I could picture that same scenario as part of my future, but don't think I can." He sighed. "I was thinking that there might be something between us, something that could develop, but I'm just not sure. I don't think I can be that guy in your scenario."

He looked up and saw her sitting there with her jaw nearly on the floor. She set her cup on the table and stood. "Really? And who asked you to be that guy? We've known each other for a matter of days and while I'll admit I'm attracted to you, I'm certainly not ready to walk down the aisle with you. I was just sharing a dream. Something that I'd like to have in the future with *someone*. I wasn't singling you out. Honestly, Riley, you need to get over yourself. I'll see you in the morning." She strode toward the door with Star at her heels.

The heat started in his chest and rose quickly to cover his neck and cheeks. Well-deserved heat to go along with his complete embarrassment. He groaned and dropped his face into his hands. He was an idiot. Pure and simple.

What was it about this woman that made him trip over his words like did when he was around her? Why did he wind up looking like a fool whenever he opened his mouth about any other topic besides business? He really had to work on that.

His phone buzzed.

His mother's text flashed across the screen.

Asher's very agitated. Wants to see you. Can you come in the morning?

Yes. I can come now.

No, in the morning is fine. He just drifted back off to sleep.

Text me if he wakes. I'll come whenever he needs me to.

See you in the morning.

His heart heavy, his mind in turmoil, Riley wanted to hit something. Or go for a very long run.

Harper and the team would have to search

in the morning without him. His nephew came first.

But he owed Harper an apology.

And he didn't want her to walk back to her room alone. He jumped up and rushed for the door. And stopped.

She was standing just inside, arms crossed, watching him. He raised his brows and she shrugged. "Someone's trying to kill you."

"And doesn't care if you get in the way."

"So you were rushing to escort me back to my room?"

"Couldn't hurt."

"Right."

Star shifted and he looked down at the shepherd then back up at Harper. *Apologize!*

"I can't be a part of the search in the morning. My mother texted and said Asher needs me."

She frowned. "Is he all right?"

He explained the conversation with his mother.

Harper nodded. "Of course. I'll go with you and the others can start the search. If you give them some direction."

"I can do that, but you don't have to go."

"I think I should. Extra eyes, remember?"

"I remember."

Apologize! He really should, but the ice in

her eyes made him wonder if she'd even hear it. Or accept it. Uncertainty made him pause. And then it was too late. She turned on her heel and walked out the door.

Riley sighed and caught up with her again. "Hey, hold on a second, will you?"

She didn't bother to turn. "What?"

"I'm sorry. I'm a jerk. An idiot. A presumptive—"

"I get it. Apology accepted. Now let's get inside somewhere so that no one can take shots at us again."

She swiped the key card and shoved the door open. He followed her inside and shut it behind him. "I shouldn't have assumed—"

"No, you shouldn't have, but it's done, you've apologized, we can move on."

"Can we?" Because now he found himself regretting his words. Not that he was ready to walk down the aisle with her any more than she apparently was with him, but dinner out with her might be nice, along with good conversation, good food... "I spoke without thinking—or perhaps, I was just overthinking. I do like you, Harper, a lot."

She continued to meet his gaze without blinking.

He sighed and raked a hand through his hair. "Can we be friends and not let the attraction that's between us interfere with what we've got to do to catch Jake and Van?"

"What attraction?" she asked, her words frigid.

He simply looked at her and her eyes thawed slightly. "Look, I get it, Riley. You've got a killer to catch and I've got a possible traitor to bring in. You're right. We need to focus on that and not let anything else distract us. Especially not a possible mutual attraction."

"Possible?"

"Possible."

He chuckled softly. "Good. Right. Exactly." He was relieved she felt the same way. Wasn't he?

"So…good night."

He frowned. "But we're still friends. We can still work together, can't we?" He had no idea why he needed her reassurance on that. He did know it wasn't just because she was his "in" to the best FBI resources that could possibly help him find Van. No. It was more than that. Way more.

Now she smiled. "Of course we can. Friends it is."

She held out a hand and he shook it. When she let go, he wanted to grab it back and tell her he didn't mean any of what he'd just said. But he couldn't. He owed it to his sister and

Asher—and any other innocent women who might stumble into Van's path—to catch him and put him away. So, he simply inclined his head and walked out the door.

He could feel her behind him, watching. And then he was in his room.

Safe.

And alone.

And not nearly as happy as he thought he'd be. As he *should* be. With one more glance out the window, his gaze probing the shadows beyond the parking lot of the motel, he let out a weary sigh. He didn't have time to be distracted and Harper was one huge distraction. *Focus, Riley, focus.*

Where are you Van?

"I'm going to find him, Charlotte," he murmured to the empty room. "I'm going to find him."

He just prayed he kept his wits about him because if Van found him first, Riley was a dead man.

NINE

Early the next morning, Harper, Star and Riley took off for Denver, while Max and Ian and the others headed for the national park to continue the search. The chopper was already in the air and searching in a grid-like pattern. Max promised to update her hourly.

Harper kept her cool where Riley was concerned. He was right. He had jumped to some huge assumptions. The problem was, he'd hit close to the mark. She *had* pictured him in the role of boyfriend then possible husband so when he'd said that role wasn't for him, she'd been hurt and embarrassed for allowing her thoughts to even go there.

What made her even more unsettled was that she didn't normally do that kind of thing. She didn't put men she met or worked with in that role. She simply…didn't. So to do that with Riley was not only surprising, it made her nervous.

But she'd keep her mouth shut and just pretend last night hadn't happened. Riley seemed willing to follow her lead. The drive to Denver passed quickly with Riley at the wheel and Harper watching for anyone who might decide to follow them and finish what he started the day before. But she didn't spot anyone and she soon found herself following Riley into the hospital.

"Are you all right?" she felt compelled to ask. While he'd said some things that sparked her ire, she still cared about what he was feeling.

He held the door for her. "Why?"

"You're tensed up and your jaw looks like it's been poured in concrete."

He ran a hand over his jaw and sighed. "I'm worried about Asher, my mother. The future."

"I can understand that."

"But I'm trying not to."

"God's got this. Try to trust that He's got a plan in all of this."

His expression softened slightly. "That's what I keep telling myself. It's sure hard to believe it, though."

"Yeah, I know."

They made their way to Asher's room and found the little guy awake and coloring while his grandmother dozed in the chair beside him. Crayons littered the floor around her and Harper wondered if they'd just missed a tantrum.

Riley's mother opened her eyes at their entrance and drew in a deep breath. Relief stamped itself plainly on her face. "Asher, look who's here."

Asher looked up and as soon as he saw his uncle, his frown flipped into a huge grin. "Uncle Riley, you came! Mimi said you were coming, but I didn't believe her."

"Well, if Mimi said it, it has to be true." He bent over and kissed his nephew on his head then rested a hand on his small shoulder.

Asher's gaze landed on Harper. "Who are you?"

Harper stepped forward and smiled warmly. "I'm Harper. I'm a friend of your uncle's."

Riley nodded to the older woman. "This is my mother, Maria Martelli."

"Nice to meet you," Mrs. Martelli said.

"And you." She shook hands with his mother then clicked her fingers and Star settled at her side. "I brought another friend, too."

Asher's eyes rounded and his jaw dropped. "A dog," he breathed.

"This is Star."

"Hi, Star."

Harper pointed. "Go tell Asher hello."

Star walked over to Asher and nudged his hand with her nose.

Asher laughed and scratched the animal's ears.

Riley's eyes caught hers and she thought she saw a sheen of tears there before he looked back at Asher. "What's on the schedule for today?"

"Another X-ray to make sure the bullet hasn't moved," his mother said. "Then we'll take him outside if he feels like it."

"I feel like it."

Riley patted Asher's shoulder. "Great. So, Champ, what happened with all the crayons?"

Asher lowered his eyes. "I threw them."

"Why?"

"'Cuz I was mad."

"Mad because you can't get off this bed?"

Asher shook his head.

"Then what?"

"Mad because my mom went away and Mimi said she wasn't ever coming back. She said she was dead and in heaven with Jesus."

Harper winced and almost felt guilty for witnessing the intimate moment between the grieving family.

Riley swallowed then cleared his throat. "I know. It makes me mad, too, but we're going to get the man who…made her go away."

"And put him in jail?"

"Yes."

"And Star is trying to help," Harper said.

Asher turned his attention to her. "She is?"

"Yes. She's specially trained to track down people like the man who hurt your mom."

"How?"

Harper explained it to him in simple terms and he listened, the rapt expression on his face touching her. "So, hopefully, tomorrow, when we go looking, we'll find him."

Asher nodded. For the next two hours, she and Riley entertained the child while his grandmother took a much-needed break. Asher finally yawned and his eyes grew heavy. "Can Star get up on the bed?"

Riley raised a brow at Harper who shrugged. She patted the foot of the bed and Star hopped up, turned three times then settled her head on her paws. Asher giggled. "There's a dog in my bed, Uncle Riley."

"And she can stay there until you go to sleep."

"'Kay. Thanks." Riley held Asher's hand until the boy went to sleep.

Harper's phone buzzed and she glanced at the screen. "It's Max," she whispered.

"Have they found anything?"

She read the message then said softly, "They found several camping areas that could have been used by Jake or Van, but said nothing concrete. He did find one person who thought she recognized Jake's picture so he feels like he's still in the area."

"Good. What about Van?"

"Nothing so far."

He frowned and nodded. "All right. When my mother gets back, let's grab a bite to eat and get back to it."

"Are you sure you want to go? Asher seems to do much better when you're here."

Conflict raged in his eyes and he sighed. "I need to do this. Asher understands. He's six, but he's smart."

"Catch him, Uncle Riley. I'll be okay."

Harper turned to see Asher's sleepy eyes on them. Riley leaned over the child. "Are you sure, Champ? Because I'll stay if you want me to."

"I want you to stay, but I want the man who killed my mom to be in jail more. I won't throw any more crayons."

Riley kissed Asher's forehead and swallowed hard. "All right, then," he said, his voice hoarse, "I'll get him and get back to you. Deal?"

"Deal."

"And you can throw the crayons if it makes you feel better."

They fist-bumped and Asher's eyes closed again.

* * *

Emotions ran across Riley's face and Harper almost thought she might be able to feel sorry for Van Blackman if Riley got his hands on him.

Almost.

The door opened and Riley's mother took her place back in the chair and picked up her knitting project.

Harper's phone buzzed again and Harper couldn't stop the gasp that slipped from her lips when she read the message. Then she smiled.

"What is it?" Riley asked.

"Good news."

"What kind?"

"You'll see. You should know in just a few minutes."

Riley's brows rose. "Now I'm really curious."

But she wouldn't tell him and he finally shot her an amused smile and leaned his head back against the chair. Star shifted onto her side and closed her eyes.

Harper was too excited to even think about dozing and if that doctor didn't get himself in the room in the next few minutes, she thought she might burst.

Just when she was ready to go find him, the

door opened and the doctor she'd been thinking about stuck his head in. "Mr. Martelli, do you have a minute?"

Riley exchanged glances with Harper and she shrugged, but that smile on her face didn't fade and the twinkle in her eyes made him wonder what she knew that he didn't.

His mother stood as well. The doctor pulled back into the hall and Riley and his mother followed him. Harper rose, but didn't follow.

"Come on out here," Riley said. "You can hear whatever he has to say so I don't have to repeat it."

Harper gave a slow nod and her heart lurched at the notion that he wanted to keep her in the loop about Asher.

Once she joined them in the hall, the doctor gave them a broad smile. "We're taking Asher to surgery."

Riley gasped. "What?"

His mother gripped his forearm and gave a small cry. "When?"

"You've got ten minutes then we're rolling him down."

Riley looked at Harper. The grin on her face rivaled that of the doctor's. "You knew, didn't you?"

"Yep."

"But...how?"

"Let me make a phone call." She had whoever she was calling on speed dial.

"This is Dylan."

"Hi Dylan, I just wanted to let you know that the doctor just told Riley and his mother that Asher's going to get his surgery today."

"Oh, yeah? Hey, that's great!"

"You want to explain how that came about?" She smiled at Riley.

"Am I on speakerphone?"

"Yes."

He laughed. "The team overheard a conversation Riley had with his nephew and decided to take action to get him up and moving. A couple of days ago, I talked to Mrs. Martelli and asked what it would take to get Asher the surgery." His mother pressed her fingers to her lips and nodded. "She gave me the details and I took it from there. Riley, you've brought us really close to finding Jake Morrow so the powers that be felt you earned the reward money. We Tactical K-9 folks pooled our resources and held a fund-raiser here at headquarters the day before yesterday. A lot of us called in favors and asked for donations. We raised the money in a little less than sixteen hours plus enough for some after-surgery costs like physical therapy."

Riley swiped a hand across his eyes. He didn't even care that tears dripped from his chin as well. "I don't know what to say."

His mother swatted him on the arm. "I think thank-you is a good start."

"Yes, yes, of course. Thank you. I'm just blown away."

"We can do that, too, but only to the bad guys. This was definitely a team effort to help the good guys, so keep us updated on his progress, will you?"

"Absolutely."

"Thanks, Dylan, talk to you later."

"Bye."

Riley pulled Harper into a hug and held on while he tried to get his emotions under control. The doctor walked off with a new spring in his step and his mother slipped back into Asher's room leaving him alone with Harper in the hallway.

Harper, who was still in his arms.

"Oh, sorry." He stepped back, stunned at the realization he'd reached for her without thinking twice about it.

"Don't be." She studied him, the look on her face unreadable.

He cleared his throat. "I'm going to stay here. It's going to be a long night."

"Of course." She grabbed his hand and

squeezed. “I’ll check with Max, but I’m sure he’ll tell me to stay with you.”

The hair on Riley’s neck stood on end and he froze. Then looked up to see Van Blackman watching from the end of the hall. The man met his eyes, saluted then disappeared through the door with the exit sign above it.

“Blackman’s here.” He raced down the hall, passing the startled nurses and hit the stairwell at a run. It vaguely occurred to him he should have checked to make sure Van wasn’t standing there simply waiting to shoot him when he came through the door, but at this point, he didn’t care. The man had shown up on his nephew’s floor.

“Riley!” Harper’s shout didn’t slow him. He continued down the stairs and out the door at the bottom. He held it open while he scanned the area. The hallway to his right held a patient on a gurney and two medical personnel standing next to him talking. The hallway to his left led to the parking garage.

Harper caught up to him and he headed for the parking garage. Then stopped. “Where’d he go?”

“I don’t know,” Harper said.

“What if he doubled back?” he gritted.

Riley turned on his heel and sprinted back up the stairs, taking them two at a time. Harper followed him once again, on her radio, and asking for backup.

Once back on Asher's floor, Riley beelined for his nephew's room.

He rushed inside to find it empty. "He's got them."

"No," Harper said, trying to catch her breath. "Don't jump to that conclusion. They were coming to get Asher for his surgery, remember?"

Riley turned on his heel and headed for the nurse's desk. "Lisa. Did they come get him? Asher? From room 312?"

"Hey Riley, what's wrong?"

"I need to know where Asher is. *Now.* Please."

"Sure." She sat in front of the computer and time slowed to a snail's pace while she clicked the keys. Finally, she looked up. "Yep. He's in the surgery prep area."

Riley's knees nearly buckled with relief. "And my mother? She's with him?"

"Um. I would assume so."

"No. I can't assume. I need to know."

She must have sensed his intense distress because without another word, she picked up the phone and dialed an extension. "Hey, is Maria Martelli down there with Asher? Uh-huh. Okay, thanks." She hung up. "She's there."

Riley dropped his head into his hands. They were fine. He wasn't going to lose them to Blackman's evil. "Okay, thank you." *Thank you, God, thank you.*

Officers arrived on the floor and Harper directed them to follow Riley. He led them down to the surgical area and found his mother reading a book to Asher who didn't seem to be paying much attention.

It took a moment to get his heartbeat to slow. In its place, fury churned. He tamped it down and forced himself to think logically, clearly.

What was Van doing here?

"We'll have someone stay on Asher and your mother from here on out."

"Yes. I think that would be a good idea."

And then Asher was being rolled back for surgery and Riley prepared himself to wait while others hunted the man who'd gotten away yet again.

TEN

Harper stood at the door of the waiting room and watched Riley sleep. Or rest. Or pray. Whatever he was doing, he had his eyes closed. His mother sat across from him working feverishly on a blanket. Her needles clicked in a soothing rhythm while the television above her head scrolled the stock market report.

Harper slipped into the chair beside Riley and he turned his head to look at her. "Did they find him?"

"Not yet," she said. "The chopper pilot spotted something and sent them to investigate, but it turned out to be a false alarm."

He sighed. "They won't find him. Not until he's ready to be found." He frowned. "Don't you need to be out there looking for Jake?"

"I updated Max on the situation and the fact that Blackman was seen here at the hospital. He told me to stay and find out what I could."

"And?"

"We've got Blackman on video."

She'd made sure Riley's family was covered and safe then gone to check with hospital security about getting a look at the video footage. It had taken five minutes to bring up the picture of Van standing in the hall next to the stairwell door. They'd tracked him back to a handicapped parking spot where he'd pulled in and placed the tag on his rearview mirror before getting out of the green pickup and walking into the hospital.

"The tag on his vehicle was stolen from a Laundromat this morning. We got him on video there, too."

"Why do you think he was here at the hospital? Looking for me?"

She fell silent then gave a slight shrug. "I have my theories."

"Such as?"

She bit her lip then sat beside him. His mother continued to knit, but Harper figured she wasn't missing a word.

Riley waved a hand giving her permission to speak her mind in front of his mother. Harper lowered her voice anyway. "You said Blackman vowed to kill you."

The needles fell silent.

"Yes."

"Because he knows he'll never be able to

stop looking over his shoulder. You've promised to bring him to justice no matter how long it takes."

Riley gave a short nod.

"So, that leads me to believe his only recourse is to kill you."

Another nod from Riley.

Harper bit her lip and shrugged. "I think Van might have been trying to get to Asher or your mother."

"But why?"

"I'm not sure. Again, I have theories, but that's all they are."

"I think he's mocking me."

"Could be that."

"It's why he's stayed around close by. I mean, why not flee the country? Why stay less than two hours away from where your victim was killed?"

"He wants Asher," his mother said softly.

Riley stilled. "*What?* Why would you say that?"

"He was crazy about that boy, you know that."

"Yes, but—"

"I think Asher's why he had such trouble letting go of Charlotte. He lost his first wife and child and once Charlotte started having second thoughts about him, it sent him into a tailspin.

He'd already gotten attached to Asher and if Charlotte left him, it would be like losing his wife and child all over again. He begged, he pleaded, he threatened. And when none of that worked, he lost it and killed her." She paused. "I think he had every intention of taking Asher from her that day and disappearing. Only the fact that he was shot, too, kept him from taking him."

"What makes you say that?"

"Charlotte told me he'd threatened that if she left him, he'd take Asher."

Riley gaped at her. "And you didn't think I needed to know that?"

"Well, since Asher was in the hospital and paralyzed—and Van had disappeared, I didn't think it was that important." She bit her lip. "Now I think it's possible he's just been biding his time."

Riley looked away and rubbed his chin. "Maybe."

"It's a good analysis, Mrs. Martelli," Harper said. "Maybe you should apply to work for the FBI." She kept her tone light in the heavy atmosphere.

The woman gave her a sad smile. "It's just called experience."

"Yeah." Harper sank into the seat next to her and joined them in the wait.

For the next six hours, they alternated pacing, dozing, sipping decaf coffee and waiting for the hourly updates on Asher's progress.

A nurse appeared in the doorway and Riley shot to his feet. She held up a hand. "Asher's doing great. The bullet has been removed and they're patching him up now."

Riley blew out a breath and slumped back down into the chair. "Thanks."

"The doctor will be out shortly to talk with you, but it's looking good for Asher."

Riley swallowed and nodded, not even bothering to try to hide the sheen of tears in his eyes. His mother clasped his hand and Harper placed hers over theirs and squeezed.

Finally, the doctor stepped into the waiting room. He removed his surgical mask and gave them a smile accompanied by two thumbs up. "It went perfect. Asher did amazing. The bullet was right where the X-ray showed. It didn't do any damage to the spine, but the tissue around it was so inflamed, it was what temporarily paralyzed Asher. Now that it's gone, once the inflammation goes down and the incision heals, I think there's real hope he'll be able to walk again soon."

His mother began to cry and Riley wrapped an arm around her shaking shoulders. "God came through," she whispered. "Thank you, Jesus."

Harper's phone rang and she stepped away to answer. "Hello?"

"It's Max. Today was a bust. Mostly. We did find someone who recognized Jake from the park's general store, but couldn't tell us where he was camping or if he was still around."

Harper rubbed a weary hand across her eyes. "When did the person see him?"

"Yesterday morning."

"All right. So, I guess we continue going on the assumption that he's staying put for now."

"Yes, but I'm not sure how long that will last," Max said. "He knows we're here looking for him."

"Is there any indication that Penny has left the area?"

"Nothing. No hits on her passport or credit cards."

"Then Jake's probably not going anywhere, either. We need to keep searching."

"I agree. Can you join in first thing in the morning?"

"I can. Where do you want to meet?"

He told her then said, "I've got a vehicle for you. It's being driven here overnight and you'll have it first thing in the morning."

"Perfect." That would help. As much as she

knew Riley didn't mind them using his truck, the official vehicle would make things easier all around.

"Now, how's Asher? The team is begging for an update."

She filled him in.

"Glad to hear the boy's doing well. We'll see you in the morning."

"See you then."

When she returned to the waiting room, Riley was pacing and his mother had resumed her knitting. He enveloped her in a hug as soon as he spotted her. "He's going to walk again."

"That's the prayer." She breathed in his masculine scent and found she didn't want to leave his arms. The thought unsettled her.

But she felt powerless to move away.

He finally let her go and cleared his throat. "I'm glad you're here."

She smiled mistily. "I am, too." She settled into the chair beside him. It was going to be a long night.

Harper and Star arrived in the national park just as the sun rose in a brilliant splash of oranges, reds and yellows. Riley pulled in beside her. He'd insisted on driving his truck just in case he had to leave fast and get back to Denver and Asher.

He climbed out of his truck and into the passenger seat. "I never get tired of watching that."

She agreed. The sight nearly took her breath away and she paused for a brief moment to simply savor it.

"Amazing, isn't it?" Riley asked softly.

She nodded. "Absolutely incredible." She paused. "Are you sure you're okay being here instead of with Asher?"

"I'm sure. The doctor said even though Asher is doing fine, they're keeping him sedated while his back heals a bit. He won't know I'm not there and Mom will call if anything comes up. I've got my truck, I'm good."

"All right, then."

He patted the leather armrest. "Nice wheels."

"Only the best for us," she drawled.

He looked at her. "You're not a typical agent, are you? Or group of agents, I guess I should say."

She blinked. "What do you mean?"

"I mean, you're more subtle. You have amazing resources, Max is the leader of your team and he calls the shots, but…" He shrugged. "I don't know. You just seem different than other agents I've known." He snapped his fingers. "For example, you don't have partners. You all work together as a team."

"Nice observation."

"So, what are you?"

She smiled. "Exactly what you see, Riley, I promise. We are special, yes. We do more classified work, I suppose, than other agents. And we have the incredible resources you mentioned. So, yeah."

Max and Ian pulled in beside them, cutting off the explanation. Max rolled down his window and did the same. "Just got a call," Max said. "Jake's been spotted."

Harper tensed. "Where?"

"Over near a campground where some kids are."

Riley blanched. "I wonder if that's the group Asher's teacher referred to while she was visiting Asher."

"Could be," Harper said.

Max shoved his Suburban in gear. "Let's head that way."

"I'll just ride with you," Riley said.

A short time later, she pulled into the campground and noticed the cabins located to her right situated into a nice circle. A building sat in the middle and she assumed that to be the bathhouse. Various vehicles were scattered about and someone had set up an area with a stage and bleachers.

Max and Ian pulled in beside her. First they'd talk to the leaders of the camp and try to get a good idea where Jake had been spotted. Then the searching would commence once again.

Harper stepped out of the vehicle and let Star out of her area. A bell rang and children began to come from the cabins. Harper judged them to be between eight and twelve years old. A few caught sight of her and pointed.

A young woman dressed in jeans and a pull-over hoodie spotted her and smiled. It was the same woman she'd seen walking out of Asher's hospital room the other day. She walked toward Harper. "Hi. I'm Beth Smith."

Harper shook the woman's outstretched hand. "I'm Special Agent Harper Prentiss and this is Star. I think you know Riley."

"Pleasure to meet you." Ms. Smith looked at Riley. "And good to see you again, Riley. How's Asher?"

"Doing well." He gave her the short version of how the surgery came about.

"That's wonderful," she said. "I'm so happy to hear that."

Max and Ian and their dogs finally joined them. After Harper made the introductions, she said, "I hear you spotted a man we're looking for."

Ms. Smith rubbed her hands together and looked around. "Yes. He was down near the river getting some water. One of the children and a chaperone, Gary, spotted him. Gary had been in the general store in Drum Creek and saw the news flash on the television that you were looking for him. He told me and we looked up the number and called it in."

"We appreciate that. Could we speak to the chaperone who saw him? Gary, right?"

"Right. He's in the second cabin on the right just past the bathhouse. He'll be helping some of the younger children get ready for the day. We're doing an early morning swim. The brave ones who want to, anyway. It's too cold for me."

"Thanks again," Max said.

They went to the cabin and knocked on the door. A little boy about nine years old opened it. His eyes widened when he saw them. "Dudes! It's the 5-0! And they've got dogs!"

Within seconds, they were surrounded by ten eager boys ranging in age from eight to ten. Harper and the others let them pet the animals for a moment before their chaperone moved them back into the cabin then stepped outside. "Sorry about that."

"Not a problem," Harper said, flashing him a warm smile.

"Are you Gary?" Max asked.

"I am. You people are fast."

"We're here with one purpose. To find our

agent and bring him home," Max said. "So what can you tell us?"

"He was down by the river. I think he was filling a canteen. When he looked up and saw me, he just nodded and walked away."

"Which way?" Max asked.

"North."

"What was he wearing?"

"A pullover sweatshirt and jeans. And he had a ball cap on."

Harper frowned. "And you recognized him?"

"Well, he took the hat off and dunked his head in the water before he pulled the hat back on. That's when I realized who he was."

Max looked at Harper. "We'll head north. You go south just in case he made a U-turn somewhere. Stop everyone you see and show his picture. We'll do the same. Use the radios to stay in touch."

"Got it."

She and Riley headed back to her vehicle while the children and their leaders made their way to the lake for a chilly morning swim.

"Riley?"

He stopped and Harper saw Ms. Smith motioning him back to her. He shrugged. "I'll meet you at the truck in a minute."

Harper nodded and led Star to the Suburban

where she turned on her radio. She fitted the earpiece into her right ear. "You guys there?"

"We're here," came Max's instant response. "Are you headed out?"

"Almost. Riley's talking to one of the chaperones. I'll check in shortly."

"10-4."

She looked back to see Riley and the teacher still deep in conversation about thirty yards away. Probably about Asher. They had their backs to her, Riley's dark head bent over hers. The woman placed a hand on his arm and Harper stiffened. Was that really necessary?

She grimaced. She was *not* jealous. She had no right to feel sharp pangs in her gut at the sight of them together. But come on…would the woman ever stop talking? They weren't in a hurry per se, but Harper was ready to get on with the search. She shot the two one more glance and saw them step into the nearest cabin.

"Great."

Harper turned her attention to Star who seemed restless. She paced to the front of the vehicle then back. "What is it, girl?"

The dog sat at her feet and leaned against her. Harper scratched her ears then opened the door for her to hop in. At first Star didn't seem to want to cooperate, but at Harper's urging, she complied. Harper shut the door and reached for the driver's handle. She'd wait for him in the truck; she liked to do her sulking in private.

A cold blade at the base of her throat froze her. "Jake?" she whispered.

"Actually, no. Try Van."

A chill slithered through her. "What do you want?"

"Where's your boyfriend?"

"Excuse me?"

"Riley!" Van yelled. "Where is he? He's always with you, but you're getting ready to leave and he's nowhere to be seen."

Her gaze flicked to the cabin where Riley was and prayed he stayed put. "He's with some of the other agents. He won't be alone. He'll always have someone on him from now on. You won't be able to get to him so you might as well remove that knife from my throat."

Van cursed. A low, menacing slew of words that expressed his severe displeasure. The hand that held the blade was steady. Decisive. She didn't dare yank away. "Well, then, I guess I get to move on to plan B," he finally said.

"Which is?"

"Your friends get you back when I get Riley."

"You're going to kidnap a federal agent?" She grasped her keys in her right hand and let her thumb rove over the controls of the remote.

"Looks that way, doesn't it? Now move before those kids get back and someone has to get hurt."

He reached around her to open the driver's door and she took a chance. She pressed the button that would release Star. The door swung open on command. The knife slipped, nicking her skin, but she ignored the sharp pain, dropped the keys and grabbed Van's wrist that held the knife against her throat.

"Attack!" She yanked his arm, the knife moved from her throat by a mere inch, and Star dove for his leg.

Van cried out and went down. Harper spun away from him. He swung the knife at Star, but the dog moved at the last minute and by chance, he missed. But Harper could see his intent to stab the animal.

"Star, release. Come now!" And just like in their training exercises, the dog released her victim and darted to Harper's side.

Harper pulled her weapon, but Van was stumbling away. "Stay put, Van!"

He ignored her and continued his fast limp-jog away from her. She could send Star after him, but he still had the knife in his hand and Harper wouldn't take a chance he'd try to stab Star again.

"Harper? What's going on?"

Riley had come out of the cabin and was running toward her. "Get in the car!" She pressed the button on her radio as she raced after Van, Star at her side. "He's here. Van Blackman showed up and attacked me. I'm fine, but he's getting away."

The roar of an engine caught her attention and she crested the hill to see a green pickup speed away, down the dirt trail, kicking up dust as he went.

"He's heading east. I'm going to try and follow him." It took a few precious seconds to get Star back in the vehicle as well as Riley, but she finally was on the road Van had just taken.

And there was no sign of him.

"What happened?" Riley asked.

"Van showed up and attacked me." She made a sharp right turn to stay on the dirt road.

"He did what?" She heard the venomous tone in Riley's voice.

"He caught me by surprise while you were in the cabin with Ms. Smith. Where is he?" she muttered, seeing nothing to indicate the direction he'd gone. "How does he just disappear like he does?" She slowed, unsure where to go.

"He could have turned off any of the little side roads along here," Riley said. "There's no way to tell which one he might have chosen."

"Harper?" Max asked, his voice coming over the earpiece.

"He's gone," she told them, seething at once more losing the man. It was now personal for her, too. "We're heading back toward Riley's truck."

"10-4 on that," her boss said. "See you in a few minutes."

Riley's phone rang, and he sighed even as he snagged it. "It's my mom." He pressed the button to connect the call. "Hello?"

Ten minutes later, Harper stood beside the vehicle with her weapon at her side while Riley spoke on the phone with his mother. It didn't appear that anything was wrong, she was just passing on an update.

Max and Ian arrived. Max stepped out of the Suburban and came to her. "Are you all right?"

She waved a hand and holstered her weapon. "I'm fine."

In the side mirror, she examined the nick in the side of her neck. It still seeped blood but wasn't deep enough for stitches.

"What happened?" Max demanded. "You said Blackman attacked you?"

"Yeah. He was there at the cabins. Riley and Ms. Smith were still talking so I went on to the truck. They stepped into one of the cabins and Van came up behind me and held a knife to my throat. He was going to take me as a hostage and trade me for Riley. I decided I didn't like that plan and changed it for him."

She rummaged in the truck and found the first aid kit.

Riley had hung up and was listening to the end of her explanation. He blanched and punched a fist into his opposite palm. "Unbelievable. The man has no fear that he'll be caught."

He took the antibiotic cream from her and used a gauze pad to clean the area then apply the cream. She winced at the sting but didn't move. He was seething but his touch was gentle. She looked into his eyes and saw the conflict raging inside him.

"We barely touched the surface of our initial search before your call came in," Max said. "We'll head north again and you two stick to the original plan and go south."

Harper nodded. "Got it."

Riley affixed a band aid over the area and closed the kit.

"Then let's find these guys and end this thing," Ian said.

Riley nodded. "I'm all for that."

Harper went ahead and transferred her equipment into the new Suburban.

The dogs sensed they were going back to work and nearly vibrated with excitement.

Max slammed his door and rolled his window down. "Stay in touch with the radios and let us know if you need backup. We'll do the same."

Harper let her eyes focus on the area where they would search. "I had Blackman in the palm of my hand and he slipped away to disappear in this massive area. It's going to be like a needle in a haystack."

Max blew out a breath. "Yes, but it's the only option we've got for now. Jake's out there, too." He paused then shook his head. "It's brilliant, really. Tons of places to hide. Lots of open areas to see if someone's coming. Yep. If I were wanting to slip off the radar, this is exactly the type of place I'd pick."

"Well, we know Van's around here," Ian said. "Let's see if we can find them both. I'm ready to head home."

Harper held out the bag that had Jake's baseball cap to Star. The dog sniffed it and lifted her nose. She started walking so Harper and Riley fell in behind her. "See you in a while."

She and Riley walked several miles, stopping each time they came across a camper or an RV to question the occupants and to show them Jake's and Van's pictures.

On their way to the next stop, Riley took her hand. She looked up. "What?"

"Are you sure you're okay?"

"Yes, I'm sure." His concern touched her.

"I'm sorry," he murmured.

"Sorry? For?"

"For whatever part I've played in making you one of Van's targets."

Harper stopped walking and turned to face him. "Riley, stop. This is not your fault. None of it. You're tracking a criminal. It's what we do. Sometimes danger is a result. But it's not your fault."

He gave a slow nod, his eyes never leaving hers. Then he sighed. "I know that. Mentally."

"Good. You ready to keep going?"

"Sure."

Finally, after losing count of how many people she'd talked to, Harper showed the pictures to an elderly man who scratched his balding head. "I think I recognize him." He pointed to Jake. "I was coming out of the general store over in Drum Creek and ran across that fellow. He was kind enough to help me change my tire."

"Did he say what his name was?"

"Nope. He seemed to be in a hurry, so I just thanked him. I offered him a twenty and he just shook his head and told me to have a good day."

"But you haven't seen either one of these guys around the park?" Riley asked.

The old man shook his head. "No, not around here." He shrugged. "Doesn't mean they're not out here, though. Lots of places to camp. It would be easy to miss them."

"Of course." Harper put the picture away and rubbed a hand over her eyes. Then smiled. "Thank you for your time."

"I hope you find them."

"Me, too."

The man paused. "Should we be worried? Should we pack up and leave?"

Harper hesitated then shook her head. "I don't think so. They're not attacking random people. They're mostly wanting to just stay hidden and off the radar. But you'll have to make up your mind about whether you feel safe enough to stay."

He shrugged. "I'll think about it."

Harper walked off and Riley and Star followed. She turned and looked around. "You know, we're down here in the valley area where it makes sense to camp what with the fresh water streams and the lake. But what if Jake and Van are hiding out up there?" She pointed to the higher elevation area. Mountainous terrain that wouldn't be easy to navigate, but would definitely be a great hiding place.

Riley planted his hands on his hips. "It would definitely be a better vantage point to watch from and be able to see if someone was coming up—and then take cover and hide to avoid the searching."

"Star isn't signaling that Jake's been anywhere around here. I say it's time to start going up."

Riley opened the map they'd gotten from the visitor's center. "Look here." He pulled a pen from his pocket and started circling. "All of these are campsites on the map. I think we need to be seeking out places that aren't mapped. Places that are flat, close to water, with an easy route out of the park should he have to run."

"Which one? Jake or Van?"

"Both, probably."

She nodded. "All right, let's go." She clicked to Star and the three of them headed toward where they'd parked her truck. Sweat beaded on her forehead and she grabbed the water bottle from the pouch on her belt. "You know, I did my research. There are four hundred and fifteen square miles to this park. That's a lot of ground to cover."

"I know. Not to mention tons of hiking trails, camping areas and so on."

"There's got to be an easier way to do this," she said.

"Choppers would help."

"Yes, they would. But Jake knows our resources. He's not going to camp out where he'd be visible from the air." She paused. "But Blackman might. He might not realize that our resources are now yours and he might not be quite so careful about staying out of aerial sight range." She got on the radio with Max.

"Have you found anything?" he asked her.

"No, but I'd like to bring in a chopper. Could you request one to make a pass over the area?" She gave him the approximate location.

"We've got one at the Denver Airport. I'll get him out here. Give him an hour."

"Thanks, Max. We'll keep looking."

Once they were inside her Suburban, she put it in gear and rolled toward the road that would take them up as Riley had directed. "Are there camping areas up there?" she asked.

"Yes. Some. They're not quite as popular as the ones near the lake, but there are those who brave the roads to get the view."

They continued to climb, looking for anything that would resemble a place someone might decide to set up camp. She watched him from the corner of her eye as she drove. He rode in silence, his jaw tight, eyes narrowed. He radiated determination—and impatience. She understood that. She wanted this to be over with as well—and she didn't have a sick nephew she was desperate to get back to.

Harper pulled into an area designated for pictures. "If I remember correctly, there's a small creek that runs through the trees behind us. It's not exactly off the beaten path, but it's a good place to start."

"Perfect." Harper climbed from the truck and Star hopped down beside her. Harper let Star have another whiff of Jake's hat and the shepherd dropped her nose to the ground.

They walked for several minutes in silence, following Star's lead. The dog searched bushes, trees and rocks to no avail. Harper stopped. "He's not been around here."

"I don't think so, either." Riley looked around. "I know where I am."

"What?"

"I forgot about this place, but my dad used to bring me and my cousins up here. There's a shallow river that runs at the bottom of that drop-off over there." He pointed.

"There's water over there?"

"Yes. If I remember correctly."

She paused as a faint sound reached her ears. "Do you hear that?"

He listened then frowned. "Yes."

She took two steps to the right, stopped then walked to the left. "I think it's coming from that direction." She pointed to the drop-off he'd indicated just moments earlier.

"Let's check it out."

Harper hurried toward the sounds that grew louder as she approached the edge of the cliff. When she stepped to the ledge, she looked down to find it wasn't a drop-off after all. A large stream of water flowed gently at the bottom. "You were right. There's water down here." Movement caught her eyes and she gasped. "Puppies!"

Riley stepped up beside her. "What?"

"Look."

He did and tensed. "There's a bag with a hole in the side. Someone threw them down there."

"And not too long ago. There's still one in the bag." Harper started down the sloping hill and heard Riley follow her. Star beat them to the bottom and began investigating the little pups. They seemed delighted to see her and one began chewing Star's front paw. She nudged it away only to have it come back and start in again.

Star looked at Harper as though to say, "Really?"

Harper scratched the dog's ears. "It's okay, girl, they're just babies. Baby beagles. Probably only a few weeks old at most."

And someone had tried to drown them. Anger at the heartlessness of some people ate at her as she pulled the last squirming pup from the bag. She held it up to her face and it licked her nose. Another gnawed on her bootlace.

Riley snagged the third one before it tumbled into the water. The fourth sat and watched the excitement, his little tongue hanging out of the side of his mouth. "They could have drowned."

"I think that was the idea," Harper muttered.

"I didn't see anyone on the way up here. Did you?"

"No. It took them some time to chew through the bag. Whoever dumped them is long gone. I'm just glad he has lousy aim and missed the water."

"What are we going to do with them?"

"Take them with us for now."

"Take them with us where?"

"We have a K-9 training unit back in Billings. One of the things we try to do is take a puppy back from each assignment to be trained."

"That's a great thing to do."

"And now we have four here." The fourth puppy that had been sitting got up and limped toward Riley. He picked it up. "This little guy is hurt."

"He might have landed the hardest when the bag hit the ground. He might need an X-ray."

"Yeah. Let's find a vet and get him taken care of."

"As for the others, we'll see if there's a place

that takes in strays for now. Like a foster home for them. Maybe someone can keep them until it's our assignment is finished. Then we can pick them up and take them back to Billings."

Riley gave a low sigh. "Well, today was a wash."

"Not really. We rescued four little beagle pups who would have died without us. We're heroes."

"Good point." He offered her a smile that resonated within her. He kept his eyes locked on hers. "Harper…"

Her heart thudded but she refused to let him know it. "What?"

"I—"

The poor guy looked terribly uncomfortable. "What is it?"

"Would you—"

"Spit it out, Riley. What are you trying to say?"

"You're not going to make it easy for me, are you?"

"Make what easy?"

He sighed. "Would you have dinner with me?"

Dinner? He wanted to have dinner. After he'd told her that he wasn't interested in being the guy for her? He really had a lot of nerve. "Riley—"

"We can talk about the case and what the next move needs to be to find Van. And Jake."

They needed to have dinner in order to do that? Harper almost said no, then bit her tongue on the words. He might be confusing, but she was being childish. "Sure, I'd love to have dinner with you."

He blinked. "You would?"

"To talk about the case? Of course."

"Oh…right. The case. Of course."

She didn't want to talk about the case. She wanted to talk about him, be with him, soak in his presence and simply enjoy the time with him. However, uncertainty kept her from voicing those thoughts. But the butterflies in her belly had no trouble expressing their excitement about the whole idea.

Together they walked back to the Suburban, carrying the puppies. She got them settled with Star in the back when the crack of a rifle shattered the silence.

Harper dropped low and pulled her weapon. "Riley! Are you all right?"

He scuttled around the front of the truck to join her. "I'm fine."

"You sure?" Another pop sounded and a bullet hit the driver's window. More pops quickly followed and a slew of bullets shattered the inside console. Harper stayed down, but couldn't help the wince. Max was going to flip at the destruction of the brand-new vehicle. But she'd worry about that later. Right now, they just needed to make sure they didn't get hit.

"Yes, I'm fine, but I saw where he is," he answered. "I think it's Van and I'm going after him."

"How? It's wide-open from here to there. He's got a good spot behind trees and will cut you down before you take two steps."

"I know. We'll have to take the truck. Get in and hunker down."

"Riley."

"Please, Harper, help me catch him."

"All right, but we're going to move fast," she cautioned. "He's got a good angle right into the truck. He'll be able to shoot us as soon as we climb in."

ELEVEN

Riley opened the passenger door and, staying low and hopefully out of sight of the shooter, watched as Harper scooted across to the driver's side, pushing the glass off the seat. Keeping her head below the shattered window, she cranked the vehicle while Riley climbed into the passenger side.

She ordered Star to lie down on the seat. Riley knew the puppies were in the enclosed area and would be protected from any flying bullets. All she had to do was move the truck forward and she would throw off the killer's aim that allowed him to plant bullets inside the vehicle.

"Ready?" she asked.

"Yes, go."

Before she lifted her head, she pressed the gas and the vehicle shot forward. More bullets sounded, but this time pinged off the side of the truck.

Harper sat up and gunned the engine once more. Riley leaned out of the window and fired off a few rounds.

The bullets coming their way fell silent.

"There he goes!" A figure darted away. He'd been tucked behind a tree at about the same level as Riley and Harper so Riley didn't think he was above them by much.

The attacker turned and got off another quick shot. The bullet hit the truck and Harper jerked the wheel then swerved back onto the dirt road. She pressed the gas and quickly closed the distance between them and the shooter. Riley pointed. "There he is!"

"He's running now!"

"At least he's not shooting anymore!"

They had to yell over the wind blowing through the broken window.

The puppies yipped from the back and Riley knew they were being tossed around a bit. But she was driving steady now, closing in on the man who'd shot at them. It had to be Van, didn't it? Or was it Jake? The two men looked so much alike, to be truthful, he really wasn't sure who they were chasing.

It didn't really matter. Whoever it was had to be stopped.

When they could go no farther thanks to the trees blocking the way, she braked and jumped out of the vehicle. Riley did the same. A walking trail led into the trees. Several vehicles were parked along a split-rail fence, but there was no one within sight. "I'm going after him," Riley said.

Harper opened the back door and let Star out. "I'm right behind you."

"Be careful, there's a sheer drop-off not too far into those trees."

She shut the door on the barking puppies and Riley heard her bringing up the rear.

He spotted Van just as he disappeared into a copse of trees. Without pausing, he pounded after him, dodging fallen logs and woody debris. "Van! Stop! This is the end of the line!"

And then Riley heard nothing except Harper and Star behind him. She caught up to him, one hand wrapped around Star's leash, the other holding her weapon. "You find him?"

"No. And I don't know which way he went."

"There's really only two choices here," she said. "There's the walking trail that way and then through the woods to my left. Would he go off the trail?"

Riley ran a hand through his hair and felt the sweat drip down the back of his neck. "I don't know. Maybe. All I know is the longer we stand here talking the farther away he's getting."

"All right. I don't have anything that belongs

to Van so Star isn't going to be much help tracking him." She glanced at her phone. "There's still no signal. I hate to split up since we won't be able to communicate with one another."

"Let's just go hunting for him. I'll take the walking trail."

She hesitated then nodded. "Fine. But be careful. Meet back here in fifteen minutes, okay?"

Riley heard her and raised a hand to acknowledge he heard her and moved down the trail at a lope. The problem was, he wasn't sure what Van would do. Would he keep running or do something unexpected like stop and hide? Riley slowed his pace, his head swiveling, hand gripping his weapon while his heart thudded in his chest. Where was he?

He'd go off the trail. Riley wasn't sure how he knew it, but it's what he would do. He ignored the *No Trespassing* signs and hopped the fence.

Something slammed into the middle of his back and he went down to the ground hard. The breath whooshed from his lungs. A booted foot aimed toward his head and Riley threw himself to the left.

And found himself airborne then crashing down against the side of a steep cliff. Pain exploded through him as he bounced and slid.

Desperate to stop his downward descent, he threw his arms out, grasping for a hold on any tree or shrub.

He found nothing and knew if he kept going, he'd go right on down to the rocky bottom below.

Star jerked on her leash and turned with a growl.

Harper slowed and spun. "What is it, girl?" The dog lunged back toward the way they'd come. Over the years, Harper had learned Star had reasons for her behavior. "All right, you're the boss, let's go."

Star took off and Harper jogged behind her, keeping her eyes in the trees and the surrounding area. She wasn't exactly being covert and couldn't let Blackman or Morrow catch her off guard.

A harsh shriek reached her ears. "Riley!"

She picked up her pace and bolted back to the place where she'd left him only to find it empty. But Star knew where she was going and pulled Harper toward the fence. She climbed over, dropped the leash, and Star darted through the middle of the wooden fence.

She raced over to the edge of the cliff Riley had warned her about only moments ago and saw a figure dart away. "Stop! Federal agent!"

The man didn't stop and Harper didn't pursue. She raced to the edge where he'd been only moments before and looked over, heart in her throat, expecting the worst. "Riley!"

He was wedged between a bush and the trunk of a tree. Star growled and Harper whirled to see Van taking aim at her. She threw herself to the side and heard the bullet hit the ground next to her. She rolled to her stomach, raised her weapon and fired back.

Van yelled, turned and ran. Harper had no time to chase him. She had to get to Riley. She could send Star after Van, but it was possible he'd just shoot her. She couldn't take the chance. "Star, down." The animal dropped to the ground.

Still on her belly, Harper army-crawled to the edge and looked down once more. Riley was still there and he hadn't moved. "Riley, can you answer me?"

"Yeah, yeah!"

She wanted to revel in the relief, but there was no time. "Can you move?"

"Not without falling again. I'm stuck." He paused. "Which might be a good thing."

Harper wanted desperately to be able to call for help, but she had to move quickly. She had no doubt Van would be back to finish the job. "I'll be right back. I'm going to get you up."

"What are you going to do?"

"Go get some gear. Um… I'd say stay put, but…"

"You're a funny woman, Harper."

He was joking, so maybe he hadn't hit his head too hard. Harper really didn't want to leave him alone while she ran back to the truck. What if Van decided to come back while Riley was helpless? She paused then called Star over. "Guard. Guard him, girl. Got it? Stay."

The animal woofed and sat. She wouldn't move until Harper returned. But if Van came back, Star would bark and let Harper know. She took off back the way she'd come, running, but being cautious in case Van was lying in wait. Once at the truck, she made sure the puppies were safe in the temperature-controlled area that held them. They were. They'd be fine until she and Riley could get back. *Please let us get back fast and in one piece.*

The prayer whispered through her mind as she unloaded the items she needed from the back. The Suburban came equipped with a first-aid kit, rappelling gear, listening devices, tear gas and other items she would want at her fingertips should she need them.

She grabbed the rappelling gear and the first-aid kit and headed back toward Riley. Again, she carried the gear in one hand, her weapon in the other so she would be able to defend herself if necessary. It seemed to take her forever, but she made it back to the area where she found Star waiting. The dog shifted at her appearance and Harper felt sure that Van hadn't been back this way. "Good girl, Star." She set the rappelling gear and first-aid kit down and looked around for a sturdy tree that would hold her and Riley on the journey back up the side of the cliff.

She dropped to her knees to check on him. "You still there?" He looked to be about fifty feet down. Close enough to talk to, far enough to need help getting back up.

"Unfortunately."

"Anything hurt?"

"Just about everything."

"Any bleeding?"

"A bit."

Harper bit her lip on blasting him with some harsh words. "Riley, I need to know the extent of your injuries. Covering them up or acting like it's no big deal isn't helping."

"You sound like my mother when she's humoring me."

Harper quit talking. She was going to kill him just as soon as he was safe. Then again, his sarcasm and droll responses gave her hope that he was truly as okay as he sounded. As a former cop, he'd deal with this kind of thing the only way he knew how.

Exactly the way he was doing it. Covering up the fear and staying calm.

She glanced at him again. At least he was alive and, as far as she could tell, not seriously hurt. For the moment. The drop below him meant imminent death.

Harper tested several trees before she found one that she knew would hold both of them for the journey back up. She attached the safety and rappel devices then threw the dynamic-style rope over the edge. Quickly, she donned the gear including the helmet and gloves. "All right, girl," she said to Star, "let me know if anyone comes this way, all right?"

Star looked at her, her tongue hanging from the side of her mouth. She'd sound the alarm if Van or anyone else approached. Harper looked at the first-aid kit. Normally, she'd take it down with her, but since Riley indicated no serious injuries, she opted to leave it. She clipped the hook to her harness then attached the spare harness that Riley would use to the rope. "I'm on my way."

"Wait. What? You're coming down?"

"What did you think I was going to do?"

"Get help."

"I *am* help."

He went silent for a moment and she wondered if he was still conscious.

"Harper?" he called.

"Yeah?"

"My hands are cut up pretty bad. I'll need something to help hold on to the rope on the trip up."

"No problem." She'd have to give him her gloves. They were slightly big on her so maybe he could make them work.

The urge to hurry nearly overwhelmed her and she started down. Her wounded shoulder protested, but she ignored it. "Make yourself useful and watch above me to make sure Van doesn't come back and cut the ropes."

Riley flinched at the thought. He missed his weapon. Unfortunately, it had gone over with him and had hit the rocks below. Then again, with the shape his hands were in, he wasn't sure he'd even be able to hold a weapon much less fire it.

Pain permeated every pore of his body. After a quick inventory, he didn't think anything was broken, but he sure was bruised up—and his hands were raw and bleeding. His left leg throbbed with an insistence that he figured would require stitches. Assuming he made it back to the top and to a doctor. Right now he didn't dare move as he could feel the limbs on the tree beneath him bending. He felt like he was right on the lip of the small protrusion and any shifting on his part would unbalance him and send him to his death. *Please, God, don't let me die. I can't leave Asher yet. Or my mother. You know they need me. Get me out of this. I promised Asher I'd be back, that I'd be there for him. I need to keep that promise, God.*

Harper appeared over the edge once again. "Close your eyes. I'm aiming to come down beside you, but I'll probably knock some debris loose."

"Just come on down," he said. "But be careful. Please. Be careful." He turned his head slightly so he could still see her, but protect his eyes at the same time.

She jumped over the edge and swung back to the cliff, her feet lightly touching before pushing off again. She took her time, being careful, and Riley kept an eye on the ridge above her. If Van came back, all he could do was warn her. She'd have to pull her weapon and shoot him if it came down to it. And all Riley would be able to do was watch.

Pain raced through him. Up his back and into the base of his skull. His leg throbbed in time with his heart. He swallowed and continued to alternate between watching the ridge and watching her.

He couldn't believe she'd come after him. But like he'd told her when he first met her, she was different. Different, as in she pulled his heart like a magnet. If he got out of this alive, he was going to have to rethink some of his priorities.

And then she was beside him. "Hey," she said softly.

"Hey."

She immediately wrapped the rope under his arms and hooked him to her. At least now if he fell, he'd just dangle instead of die.

"We're going to have to work fast," she said. "I need to get you in the harness then we're going up before Van comes back. Can you walk?"

"Can you check my left leg?"

The fact that he'd asked must have surprised her. She raised a brow then worked her way around to his left side where she took a look and sucked in a breath. "Yikes."

"Bad?"

"Definitely not good. Hold tight, I need to get a better look."

She tugged on his pants leg and fire shot through him. "Ah!" The cry escaped him before he could smother it.

"Whoa. Sorry. Your jeans are pretty shredded and you've lost some meat, but I don't see any bones."

"No, it's not broken." He knew what *that* felt like.

"That's gotta hurt, though."

He gave a low grunt. "It hurts." As he'd just proved by being a wimp and letting out that cry.

"All right. Normally, I'd patch you up hanging here, but one: I'm very nervous about being here too long."

"And two?"

"I left the first-aid kit up above because you were only bleeding 'a bit.'"

"Understatement?"

"A *bit*."

"Yeah, sorry. Honestly, I didn't really feel the leg until you were halfway down. It doesn't matter now. Let's get out of here."

Harper unhooked the extra harness and slipped it up his legs—careful to ease it over the wounded left leg—then around his waist. She balanced on the edge of the ledge while she helped him work his way into it. His hands were a real nuisance and hurt. A lot.

But finally, they got it done.

Once he was safely harnessed and hooked to the rope, Riley drew in the first deep breath he'd taken since the fall.

"All right, let's go," he said. She pulled the rope from under his arms and handed him a pair of gloves.

"I thought these might be big enough, but I see they're not. You'll have to be creative."

He didn't bother to try to put them on. Instead he pressed them into his palms to cushion his hold on the line. Hopefully the blood wouldn't cause them to slip. He grasped the rope he was hooked to and looked up. Still no Van, but he had a feeling time was running out.

"Have you ever done this before?" she asked.

"I have to say this is one sport I've not tried, but it can't be that hard, can it?"

She shot him a perturbed look and he grinned. At least he hoped it was a grin. The pain might have turned it into a grimace.

She shook her head. "Stay with me. Slide your hands up the rope and pull yourself. One step at a time. Keep your good foot against the wall of the cliff. Can you put any weight on the injured one?"

He tried it. Again the fire burned up his leg and sent his head spinning, but he could do it. "I'll make it."

Together they made their way up the side of the cliff. One hand over the other. One foot then the next. He looked up to see Star at the edge looking over. She pranced sideways and whined.

"Get back, girl," Harper commanded. "Back."

The dog disappeared. "Guess Van hasn't shown up." Riley grunted at the next step. "Star only seems worried about you being down here."

"That's the good news."

"Is there bad news?" he asked.

"Other than the fact that he's still out there?"

"Right."

She sighed. "No. That's about it."

The world spun and darkness hovered at the fringes of his consciousness. "I hate to ask but can we stop for just a second?"

She paused and he leaned against the side, his eyes turning upward. They only had about ten feet left until they reached the top. He couldn't pass out now. The inky blackness receded slowly. He drew in breaths through his nose and let them out his mouth.

"You all right?"

Her concern touched him. "I'm all right." He drew in a fortifying breath and nodded. "I'm ready."

She didn't offer him more time.

Riley bit his lip and pushed off the cliff wall. This time while the darkness threatened, he was able to push on. It probably only took them about five more minutes to get to the top, but seemed to take forever. He soon found himself lying on the ground, staring at the blue sky and dragging in great gulps of air. His leg pulsed in time with his heartbeat, his hands throbbed and other cuts and bruises would soon make their presence known.

But he was alive. *Thank you, God, that I'm alive. Please keep me that way.*

Harper dropped beside him. She laid her gun next to him. "Just stay still for a minute."

"We need to get out of here."

"I know." She ran her fingers through his hair. "No bumps."

"Amazing enough, I didn't hit my head. Just let me be for a few seconds."

She backed off and he knew he sounded curt. He hadn't meant to.

A wet tongue swiped across his face and he turned his head to see Star watching him. "Thanks, girl." He shifted his gaze to Harper. She'd pulled off her harness and was tucking it away into the bag. "And thank you."

Harper finished zipping her harness into the carrying bag and set it aside. Star showed no sign that anything was amiss around them so Harper felt like she could focus on Riley for the next several moments. If he would let her. Now that he'd had a chance to catch his breath, she pulled out the first-aid kit and moved to kneel beside him. "So are you going to let me take a look at that leg?"

He shifted and sat up.

Then kissed her.

Harper blinked, her mind thrown into sudden turmoil at the feel of his lips on hers. However, it never occurred to her to protest. She'd grown to care for this stubborn bounty hunter and she couldn't deny she wanted to kiss him, too. So she did.

Seconds later—or maybe it was minutes—he pulled back and said, "We need to get out of here."

"Star will let us know if anyone is around."

"If Van's got a rifle and a scope, we'll be dead before Star gets a whiff."

He was right. Her worry for him clouded her thinking. She gave a mental snort. It wasn't worry that had her mind reeling. That kiss…

She cleared her throat. "Can you walk on the leg?"

"I can walk." He rolled to his feet and air hissed from between his teeth. "Won't feel good, but I can walk."

"You need stitches. Let me at least bandage it."

"No time. Van could be anywhere."

Harper tightened her lips at his stubbornness. "So you had time to kiss me, but there's no time for first aid?"

He flashed her a grin that almost hid the pain she knew he was in. "Priorities. And besides, kissing you helped more than any kind of first aid or bandages would. Now, let's go."

Harper backed off because she didn't entirely disagree with him. Not about the kissing part, but about the danger part. Although the kissing part had been really nice.

She huffed and waited for him to step out of the harness.

Then they were ready.

She tapped her hip. "Star, heel."

Star fell into step beside them and they made their way back to the Suburban. Riley moved slowly, but at least he was moving. She wasn't sure what she would have done if she'd have had to carry him.

She noticed his vigilance even as she kept her senses tuned to the area around them. Why hadn't Van returned? He wanted Riley dead and he'd had the perfect opportunity to make sure he accomplished that. The thought spun on an endless loop.

Unless…

"He thinks he killed you," she said.

She opened the passenger door of the truck

and Riley fell into the seat with a groan. "What?"

"That's why he didn't come back. He thinks you fell all the way to the bottom."

Riley went silent and she slammed the door. Star followed her around to the driver's side and hopped in. Harper stared at the dog for a moment then shrugged. There was plenty of room in the front for her, but it was a bit out of character. She knew she rode in the back. Harper glanced at the sleeping pups in Star's area and shook her head. "Don't want to be a mama right now, huh?"

Star didn't look at her.

Harper cranked the truck and pulled away from the lookout area. She planned to head straight for the nearest hospital.

And pray Van didn't come back to find Riley gone and realize he wasn't dead after all.

TWELVE

Riley looked at his leg in disgust. It had been three days since his roll off the cliff. A pearly white bandage now covered twenty stitches.

He'd lost a good bit of blood, but nothing his body wouldn't take care of in time. Drum Creek's hospital wasn't nearly as large or well-equipped as the one in Denver, but it had been able to take care of his injuries just fine and he refused to be transported to the larger hospital. Van was close by and as soon as they let him leave, he'd be on the hunt again.

He sipped orange juice and nibbled on a hamburger someone had rounded up from the small hospital cafeteria in spite of the fact that he wasn't really hungry. But the red meat was good for him and he needed his strength to continue his search.

He leaned his head back against the pillow and closed his eyes. The painkiller they'd given him was making his head swim and he'd already decided there'd be no more of those.

He'd let his mother know of the accident and that he wouldn't be able to be at the hospital for a few days. She'd wanted to drive out to see him and he'd talked her into staying with Asher. She'd finally given in, but he could tell she hadn't liked it. He figured the only thing that had kept her at the hospital was the fact that he texted or called her on a regular basis. Which was fine with him as she kept him updated on Asher. He was so thankful the little guy continued to improve with each passing day. Soon, they'd get him into therapy and up on his feet. Riley couldn't wait.

The knock on the door jerked him out of a light doze. He hadn't realized he'd fallen asleep. "Come in."

The door opened and Harper stepped inside with Star at her side. "You're being sprung."

The sight of her filled him with a quick rush of gladness. "And you're my ride?"

"You think you'll get a better offer?"

He gave a small laugh. "No. You'll do."

"Thanks." She frowned. "So how do you really feel?"

"Better physically. Mad emotionally." She lifted a brow and he shrugged. "He got away again and almost killed me in the process."

"Well. True." She ran a hand through her short hair and leaned against the sink. "Do you feel up to taking a ride or do you want me to take you back to the hotel?"

"A ride where?"

"I did some research while I was waiting to hear how you were doing and found a beagle rescue right here in Drum Creek. The woman who runs it said she'd take them in and keep them for us as long as we needed her to. Two of the puppies are very hyper. I don't think they'd do well in the training program so she's going to find forever homes for those two."

"No kidding. So where are the puppies now?"

"The team has been taking care of them for the last couple of days. I sent one to the training center back in Billings to be raised and trained as a K-9, but I've got the others in Star's area for now. It's temperature-controlled so there's no hurry to get going if you need more time."

"They gave me a painkiller a little while ago, but I think I'm all right to ride out to a beagle rescue."

"I don't mind dropping you at the hotel."

"No, I'll just brood about Van getting away." He scowled.

"All right, if you're sure."

"I'm sure. What about the little guy who was limping? Is he okay?"

"He's fine. He had a dislocated hip, but the vet was able to set it. He also provided some medication to help keep him calm while it heals. He won't work for the training program, either, so we'll just have to find a good home for him."

"Cool. Let's get out of here."

As soon as he was checked out and loaded into the Suburban that she said had been delivered the day after his tangle with the cliff, he held one of the puppies while she drove. Even with a sore hip and on medication, the little guy was full of energy and liked to nibble on his fingers. "They're cute, aren't they?" he said.

She cast a glance his way. "Adorable."

"Asher wants a puppy."

"All little boys want a puppy. Are you thinking about keeping one for him?"

He sighed. "No. Not yet. The timing is wrong." He lifted the pup and let it lick his chin. "Maybe after his surgery."

She smiled, her sympathy clearly written on her pretty face. "I think that sounds like a great plan."

Riley fell silent thinking about his sister, her son and the man who'd radically altered all of their lives. *God, if You're listening, I need Your help to catch this guy. I can't believe You don't want him to pay for what he's done.*

"Do you believe God is really just?"

Harper blinked at the question that came at her from nowhere. She shrugged. "Yes. Why?"

"Even after your childhood and everything I know you've seen while working for the Bureau? You can still believe that?"

She fell silent and thought about his questions. Then nodded. "Yes. And sometimes God doesn't have to do a thing to show it to me. I see it everywhere I look."

"What do you mean?"

"Because of the consequences that come with our actions. Sure, it seems like some people never get caught doing the wrong thing. The illegal thing. But even if the drug addict is never arrested for possession, he's still dying because of his choices. Even if the dealer isn't arrested for supplying drugs, he's still living in a world that is uncertain and death stalks him every day."

"What about the abuser that goes unpunished? The murderer that gets away with killing a mother?"

She nodded slowly. "I've thought about that, too. I don't know how—or why—I decided to think about it this way, but I tried to put myself in their mind."

"Scary."

"Sort of. I tried to think—if I made the choice to kill someone in a jealous rage like Van, how would I feel inside? Do you think he's ever known any kind of real peace since that day? He has to live with what he's done on a daily basis, minute by minute, second by second."

"Good, I hope it keeps him from sleeping, from ever knowing peace," he gritted out. "He doesn't deserve to feel peace."

"I hear you. Don't get me wrong—I believe in justice. I believe if someone commits a crime, he or she should definitely pay for it in the whole 'be-arrested-go-to-prison' kind of justice. If I didn't believe that, I wouldn't have the job I have." She released a breath. "But I'm not talking about the ones who are caught. I'm talking about the ones we don't catch, the ones that appear to have gotten away with their crime. Part of me wonders if they aren't living with a sort of punishment every day, anyway. A self-inflicted one. That living with what they've done and who they've become is retribution in a sense."

Riley didn't speak for a moment. "It's not enough."

"Yeah. I know."

"What if they feel no remorse? What if they don't care?"

"That's a whole different issue. I'm not talking about psychopaths or sociopaths. I'm not talking about people with a mental illness. I'm talking about people who are in their right mind, who do something they know is wrong and that has severe consequences. And then have to live with that the rest of their lives."

"And you think they regret what they do?" he asked.

"Yes, of course. Some, anyway. Not all. But no one starts out life saying 'I want to be a criminal and go to prison.'"

He pinched the bridge of his nose. "I don't think Van falls into that category. I don't think he has any regrets for what he's done. I think my sister served his purpose for the time they were together."

"Which was what?"

Riley sighed. "Van and I had a long conversation shortly after he and Charlotte started dating. He was an only child growing up in an abusive situation when Child Services stepped in and put him in a foster home. The first of many."

Harper shot him another glance. "You've learned everything there is to know about this man, haven't you?"

"Everything. It pays to know your enemy."

"So when he aged out of the system he went looking for a family," she guessed.

"When he was eighteen, he married a girl that was in the last foster home where he was living before he aged out. She died giving birth to his son three years later."

"Oh, me. So, that's what your mother meant when she was talking about why Van was having such a hard time letting Charlotte and Asher go."

"Yes. And then when he realized she wasn't going to get back together with him, he just… flipped, I guess." His jaw hardened. "Anyway, after his wife and son died, he seemed to jump from relationship to relationship. Two of the women I've talked to said that he was a great guy in the beginning, but soon took over their lives, smothering them, refusing to let them have friends, cutting them off from their families—and threatening to kill them if they left him. They took their chances and left."

"And he never went after them or killed them."

"No, my sister was his first. And if we don't find him, she won't be his last."

Harper digested his words. She'd known criminals like Blackman, of course. Had caught some and put them away. She also knew Riley was right. If Blackman was allowed to elude capture, he'd just disappear long enough for law enforcement to give up looking for him then continue his deadly romances. He definitely had to be stopped.

She pulled into the drive of the beagle rescue and parked in front of the barn as she'd been instructed by the woman who'd given her directions yesterday. Riley held the now-sleeping puppy tucked into the crook of his arm.

A finger stroked the pup's head and Harper thought she saw bit of wistful longing in his eyes. "You sure you want to leave him?"

Riley cleared his throat. "I'm sure." He sighed and stepped out of the vehicle.

Movement from the barn caught Harper's attention. She opened the driver's door and slid out of her seat. Her boots landed on a mixture of grass and red dirt.

A tall, dark-haired, dark-eyed woman in her early sixties approached them, hand outstretched. "Hi, I'm Justine. You two must be Harper and Riley." Harper shook her hand then Riley did the same. "So glad you brought the pups out here. We have plenty of room for them and will find them a good home."

"Not that I believe everything I read on the internet, but you had a lot of great reviews online," Harper said.

Justine laughed. "Well, you can believe those. I didn't have anything to do with them. I just make sure I have happy animals and customers. As long as I do that, the good reviews pour in. Now, let me see the babies."

Harper opened the back door and pulled the other two sleepy pups from Star's area. Star took advantage of the open door to jump to the ground. Harper noticed the shepherd had rather taken to the puppies over the last two days and thought she might miss them when they were gone.

But she'd be fine. She had work to do.

Justine scratched Star's head and the animal closed her eyes in bliss.

"You just made a lifelong friend," Harper told her.

"She's a beautiful dog."

"Thanks. I think so, too. So—" she held the two puppies in a gentle grasp "—where should we put them?"

"Follow me."

Harper and Riley did as requested and walked behind the woman to enter the barn. "There's a play area over there." She pointed to an octagon-shaped baby-gated area. Fresh chips covered the inside and held bowls of water and food.

Harper placed the puppies inside and they

immediately attacked the food and water. "Greedy little things, aren't you?" She'd just fed, watered and let them run shortly before heading to the hospital to get Riley.

"Do you have homes for them yet?" Riley asked. He still held the third puppy.

Justine rubbed the little head and the puppy tried to nip her. Riley chucked him under the chin and he turned his attention to Riley's finger. "No, not yet," Justine said, "but it won't take long. We'll get them checked out by a vet, give them their first round of shots, and by the time we're finished with the open house we have every other month, they'll be with some great forever homes."

"Good." Riley cleared his throat and finally placed the playful puppy in the pen. He yawned and padded over to join his brothers in finishing off the food and water. "He had his hip worked on, did Harper tell you?"

"She did. It's not an uncommon thing. I'll take special care of him."

"Thanks."

Harper pulled her keys from her pants pocket. "Well, I can see they're in good hands. Riley, you ready?"

He looked up from the puppy he'd still been watching. "Yeah. Sure."

"Thanks for rescuing them," Justine said. "I

don't know why it's easier to throw a sack of puppies in a river than it is to just bring them to someplace like here."

"It's sad," Harper responded. "And I can't dwell on it or I want to go hunt the heartless jerks down and shake some sense into them. Thanks for everything."

"Of course."

Harper walked out and Riley trailed behind her. "You're thinking about that puppy, aren't you?"

"What? No."

"Liar."

He smiled at her gentle rebuke. "It's just the drugs talking. I'll be fine once they're out of my system."

"Right."

The drive back to the motel didn't take long. She let Riley off with instructions to rest. The fact that he didn't argue told her he wasn't feeling quite as well as he projected.

Harper stepped inside her room and sank onto the end of the bed. Star joined her and settled her head between her paws. Harper checked in with Max and learned the others were still working in the national park, looking for more evidence that Jake was still there. She offered to join them.

"Take a break," Max said. "You'll be back on in the morning."

That was fine with her.

Harper pulled her laptop over and opened it. As she had done numerous times before, she typed in her father's name. Grant Prentiss. She knew she should just give up the search for him, but part of her couldn't. She had to know what happened to him.

When she got a notification of a new message she sat up straight.

"What's this?"

Star lifted her head and blinked at Harper.

Harper scratched the dog's ears but focused on the screen. He was wanted on drug trafficking charges.

Sickness pooled in the pit of her belly and she shut the computer. Harper stared at the wall and lost track of time while she thought about the man whose DNA she shared. She remembered yelling, fights, things crashing in the night while she hid under her bed. And then the long silences before it would all start back up again.

And then he was gone shortly before her fifth birthday.

How could she miss someone who'd never wanted her? Someone who'd hardly acknowledged her existence other than to tell her to get lost?

She shook her head and stood.

Her phone buzzed and she swiped it from the clip where it rested against her hip. A text from Riley.

I've thought of another couple of places that would work as possible hiding places in the park. Let's go tomorrow.

That's the plan. Are you going to feel up to it? she texted back.

Doesn't matter.

Of course it does. You had a bad fall. You're fortunate you weren't killed. You need to rest.

I'll rest once Blackman's behind bars. I'm going. Are you going with me?

I'm going. Max has already said we'd be searching out there again tomorrow.

What time?

First light.

See you then.

Harper texted Max to let him know Riley's idea. He responded with a thumbs-up emoji and a promise to be ready to join them.

She set the phone aside and rubbed her eyes. Another early morning. She prayed it was going to be a successful one and no one ended up shot at or dead.

THIRTEEN

Riley wouldn't complain to anyone, but he had to admit the exhaustion, in addition to the pain from the still-healing injuries, was weighing on him. His hands ached, his leg throbbed, but there was no way he was going to miss the search this morning.

He stepped out of his room to find two Suburbans parked out front. Ian and Max were ready with their dogs in the back. Harper sat in the driver's seat waiting on him. Riley opened the door and slid into the passenger seat.

"Good morning," she said.

"Morning."

"A little sore?"

"A bit," he replied.

"Did you get any rest?"

"Nope."

"You refused to take any pain meds, didn't you?"

"Maybe."

"Gotta work on all that early morning chatter, Martelli, it could get annoying."

He slid her a sideways glance. Then smiled. He couldn't help it. As crabby as he felt, he didn't want to be in a bad mood with her. "I'm sore, but I took some ibuprofen so it'll kick in soon." She looked good decked out in her gear. But she looked good no matter what she wore. He'd known a lot of physically beautiful women, but it was rare to find one with a matching beauty on the inside.

His sister had been one of those women. And Harper was one as well. It drew him like a moth to the flame. "Anyone locate my weapon yet?"

"Yes. They found it yesterday. Two park rangers covered the area where they thought it might have landed and found it."

"Is it toast?"

"Pretty much. I brought one you can use for now."

"Thanks."

While she drove, Riley prayed that today would be the day they'd catch Van Blackman. He knew the others were more concerned about Jake Morrow—and Riley knew the man needed to be caught—but Van was his priority.

Soon, Harper pulled through the gates of the park. "Which way?"

"Keep going until you see the curve that goes

up. Like the way we went a couple of days ago. Only before you get to the top, there's a turn-off to the left. I'll point it out to you when we get there."

"Keep an eye out."

"Yes, ma'am."

"And wear this." She reached into the back-seat and handed him a Kevlar vest. "No sense in taking chances."

He pulled it on, zipping it up and attaching the Velcro straps. "I'm ready when you are."

They stepped out of the vehicle and he had to admit, he felt better with the vest on. Now he could only hope Blackman continued to be a lousy shot. He grabbed his backpack from the floorboard and slung it over his shoulder with a wince. With each passing day, he discovered new aches and pains. And bruises. His legs were the worst. There'd be no shorts for him anytime soon.

Star circled Harper's leg and sat.

"We'll have to hike up the trail," Riley said. "Once at the top, we'll need to split up. There's a pretty deep river that divides the area in two. On either side there are a few more isolated places to set up camp."

Max nodded. "Ian and I can take one side. You and Harper can take the other."

Harper nodded. "Let's get going, then." She

started off and Riley fell into step behind her and Star, with Max and Ian bringing up the rear. Riley slung his rifle over his shoulder and winced again when he pulled other muscles that had been strained in his fall. His bandaged hands still hurt, but they wouldn't stop him from doing what needed to be done. His fingers, although cut and bruised as well, were free.

But that was all right. He only needed one to pull the trigger.

Harper noted Riley's quiet determination. He kept to himself, but she didn't have any trouble reading him. If he saw Van Blackman today, it was going to be over. One way or another.

She didn't blame him. It had been a long hard road for him since his sister's death. He needed closure and to be free to be with Asher.

And you?

She immediately quieted that little voice. As much as she might yearn for the right guy to build a life with, she'd made a commitment to her job. And right now that was to find Jake Morrow.

Blackman and Morrow. Both fleeing the law for various reasons. Harper didn't think the two men were hiding out together, but they'd definitely wound up in the same general vicinity.

She hoped by the end of the day, she'd have some closure as well.

They hiked up the sloping incline, passing several others enjoying the early morning sunrise. With each person they saw, she pulled out Blackman's and Morrow's pictures and showed them. With each negative response, Harper's hopes that Riley might be onto something started to diminish.

She heard the river before she saw it. When they stepped around the bend, they stopped to consider their options.

Max pointed. "We'll head this way over the bridge. You two take that side. Keep the radios on. There's no phone signal up here."

Harper nodded and clicked Star to heel. She held out the bag with Jake's hat in it to the dog and Star got the scent. Nose to the ground, she trotted along the path. She and Riley followed in silence for several minutes, listening and watching.

Star stopped. She pranced a little, sniffed again then moved toward an open clearing that looked to be a prime camping spot. Surrounded by large stone cliffs, it was tucked back from the river. They approached it with Star eagerly leading the way.

"Has she got something?" Riley asked.

"Possibly."

Riley nodded. "There's a tent and a bicycle. No sign of a vehicle."

"Can you even get one up here?"

"Yes, I've only been up here a handful of times, but there's a road that you can follow around the edge of the mountain that leads up here. But if we drove, we might miss something. Like all of the hiking paths that branch off around here."

They continued to follow Star to the edge of the campsite. Harper held her weapon ready. Then Star skirted the area and started climbing the rocks behind it. It wasn't quite as steep as it had looked from a distance. "Okay, then, if Star can do it, so can I," she muttered. "Up we go."

Harper stayed behind the dog and climbed. Loose debris tumbled behind her. She turned to see Riley working his way up as well. He placed one bandaged hand on a protruding rock and jerked back with a grimace.

"Why don't you see if there's an easier way up here?"

He scowled up at her. "I can make it."

She stopped Star for a moment and the dog waited, panting, tongue lolling over the side of her mouth. "I'm not questioning that. But it might be better if we come at this from two different angles. If he's up there, we can trap him between us."

Riley hesitated, then nodded. "All right."

He made his way back down and disappeared around the edge of the campsite. She told Star to seek and the two of them continued up the sloping cliff. It wasn't a terribly hard climb, but she was in a sweat by the time she got to the top.

She stopped and took in the view. It was gorgeous to her back, but in front of her there was a small expanse of green, then trees clogged the area. Perfect for hiding if someone got too close. She looked around for Riley, but he wasn't in sight yet. It was possible he had to walk a fair distance in order to find another route to the top.

Should she wait on him?

Star tugged on the leash, trying to get into the trees. "Star, hold."

The dog stilled, but her sides quivered with the desire to go. She had Jake's scent and wanted to follow the trail.

Harper gave one last look over her shoulder. Still no Riley. He couldn't be much longer, could he? She hated to keep waiting and give Jake a chance to get farther away. Star pulled again on the leash. "Okay, girl, we're going." She pressed the button on her radio. "Riley, location?"

"Heading your way."

"Star has Jake's scent. I'm going after him."

"Where are you?" Max asked.

She gave him her approximate location.

"Harper, wait for me," Riley said.

"Just a minute more then I'm going after him."

"I don't know how far away I am. I had to walk awhile."

She dropped a glove to the ground then leaned down to position it. "Keep coming until you see the tree line just ahead of where I climbed up. My glove is on the ground. Follow the direction of the index finger. And bring my glove with you, please."

She headed for the trees, her weapon ready. Star bolted ahead of her, straining against the leash. Harper scanned the area, watching, her nerves tense, senses alert. Star really wanted to race into the woods, but Harper didn't want to let her go. If Jake was in there and he didn't want to be found, he'd shoot the dog. And he wouldn't aim for the vest she wore. No, she'd keep Star with her where she had more control.

Star broke the tree line and Harper followed. She placed a hand in front of Star who immediately quieted. Harper stood still and simply listened. When she heard nothing, she once again gave Star the order to continue. The shepherd turned right and Harper followed.

And came face to face with Jake Morrow, his weapon aimed at her head. "Hello, Harper."

Riley had to make his way up the cliff in a roundabout way, but he finally stepped out onto the top and paused to catch his breath. He'd still had to climb, but not as much as Harper.

So, where was she?

He almost called out then figured he'd better keep the noise to a minimal level. No sense in alerting someone to the fact he was there. He held his weapon in his right hand and lifted his radio with his left. "Harper? Where are you?"

Silence.

Riley frowned. "Harper?"

Still she didn't answer. He knew she had on the earpiece that allowed only her to hear him. So why wasn't she answering?

The options weren't good. Alarm slithered through him.

He walked toward the woods and then realized he was quite a distance from where Harper would have come out at the top of the cliff. Could he simply be out of range of her earpiece? Surely, they had better equipment than that. He started the trek that would take him in her direction.

"Harper?"

Still no answer.

"Riley, is something going on?"

Max's voice in his ear. "I'm not sure. Give me a few minutes and I'll get back to you." He paused. If Max could hear and answer him, why couldn't Riley?

It took him a good five minutes more to arrive to the place where Harper would have crested the hill. But she wasn't there.

He found the glove she'd told him about and leaned over to pick it up and tuck it in his pocket. He knelt and examined the red dirt that covered the ground. A boot track that could be Harper's led toward the trees. Star's prints were also there, just slightly ahead of Harper's. Exactly as she'd told him.

He took off at a jog and was almost to the tree line when he heard the gunshot.

A split second later, fiery pain raced through his side and he stumbled to the ground. Riley lay still as he tried to breathe. But he knew exactly what had happened. Van Blackman had seen him first. Riley pressed a hand against his bleeding hip and rolled into the cover of the woods just as another bullet kicked up the dirt where he'd been lying. He shoved the top edge of his jeans down and glanced at the wound. Just a graze. It was ugly and would leave another scar to add to his growing collection, but as far as Riley could tell it was nothing too serious. Nothing that would keep him from continuing the hunt.

The gunshot echoed around them and Harper flinched. She turned. "Riley!" She started to head back toward the tree line when Jake held up a hand and jerked the weapon at her. "Keep walking." When she'd first run into him, he'd immediately taken her weapon then forced her to walk with the excuse he wanted to talk to her back at his camping site.

She'd agreed simply because she wasn't sure what he would do if she refused. Only now Riley could be in trouble and need help.

"I'm going to check on my friend."

"And I said don't move, Harper." He inched the gun up so that it pointed to her forehead.

She froze. Star did the same, looking up and waiting for Harper's next command. "What are you doing Jake? Are you going to shoot me?"

"Not unless you give me a reason to."

"Stop this. Put your weapon away and let's talk."

"Not until I'm sure you'll listen to me first."

"I'll listen, but I need to make sure Riley's all right." Riley would know something was up when she didn't answer. But she didn't want him to walk into trouble without some kind of warning.

Her radio was in her pocket. A mere click of a button would bring help. But if she moved her hands, she wasn't completely confident that Jake wouldn't shoot her. And Agent Morrow would know what she was doing. He'd once worn a radio exactly like hers once upon a time. He'd yanked the earpiece out and forced her to remove her vest and leave it, afraid she'd have some sort of tracker on it when he confronted her so if Max or anyone said anything, she wouldn't know. She did notice that he kept the radio.

"I'm not concerned about your friend. Keep going."

"That was two gunshots, Jake. He could be hurt."

"Or he could have been shooting a snake or a wolf or whatever. Walk!"

Harper's pulse continued its frantic pace but she reluctantly continued to head in the direction Jake ordered. She truly wasn't certain that he wouldn't kill her. And she wouldn't be any good to Riley dead.

But she had to try to warn the others. She slid her hand down toward the radio.

Jake jabbed the weapon at the base of her

skull. "Don't. Keep your hands where I can see them."

Harper bit her lip. This wasn't the Jake she'd known when they'd worked together. No, she hadn't liked him all that much as a person, but he'd been a top-notch agent and never hesitated to rush in to help someone in need. "What's happened to you?"

"A bad break in life."

"Can't you see that you don't need the weapon? Put it away. We've talked before without you holding a gun on me." Could he really be a double agent? She was sure leaning in that direction. Trusting him was out of the question at this point.

She bit her lip on the words and prayed that Max or one of the others was trying to get ahold of her and would know something was wrong when she didn't answer.

Finally, Jake directed her to a small shelter. An old cabin that had probably been there for decades sat up on a sloping hill that led down to the river. "Nice spot."

"I like it. Nice, quiet and private." He smirked. "And hard to find unless you know where you're going and what you're looking for."

"What are you doing here in Colorado?"

"Looking for someone."

"Penny?"

"Yeah."

He led her inside and she noted the rustic appearance. A dirt floor, the front door that didn't close all the way, open windows that could use some glass panes. A small cot with a sleeping bag lay next to the far wall.

He'd been roughing it.

Jake motioned to a chair at the round four-person table someone had made from an oak tree. "Have a seat and keep your hands where I can see them." She did and he pulled the radio out of her pocket and tossed it onto the counter. "I don't need any more company until I can convince you why I can't come in yet."

Conflict raged inside of her. "What are you saying, Jake? That you have a good reason for this wild-goose chase you're leading us on?"

She sent up a silent prayer for Riley and settled on the edge of the chair, ready to fight back if she had to.

Jake stood at the old-fashioned hand-pumped kitchen sink, his back to it, watching her with hooded eyes. He kept the gun steady on her head. Where the bullet wouldn't be blocked by her vest. "A good enough reason," he said.

"Like what?"

"Like I managed to escape from Angus Dupree after the shootout in the warehouse in Los

Angeles. But while he had me captive, Dupree threatened to kill Penny…" He met her gaze. "And my son."

The raw anger there was real. But were the words? If they were, then maybe there was a valid reason for his behavior after all. And yet, Jake had been a good agent for a reason. He was very skilled at playing whatever part he had to. "So you went after them."

"Yes. Then you guys showed up at her house and she ran."

"And so did you."

"I didn't have time to stay and explain my actions. I had to catch up with Penny."

That made sense in a weird sort of way. "And did you?"

"Yes. I told her about Dupree and the threats and sent her away. I told her I'd catch up to her later. But when I went to meet her as planned, she'd disappeared."

"That doesn't really make sense. Why not go with her?"

"I wanted to circle back and make sure no one was following her. I finally tracked her here, using informants I've made over the years. I don't trust Dupree. I'm sure he's hunting her just as I am and I'm scared to death he's going to catch up to her before I can find her and convince her that I just want to keep her and Kevin safe."

"Why haven't you asked for our help? You're a part of this team. We'd back you in a minute and you know it."

"I know. But I couldn't involve the team. This was personal. You had enough to do trying to track down Dupree and his goons. I couldn't pull your attention from that for something like this. I needed to take care of this by myself."

Now that sounded more like the Jake she knew. Or thought she knew. "I get that Penny's on the run from Dupree, but why run from you? Hide from you? It makes no sense."

He raked a hand through his hair. "She doesn't trust me. I think she's afraid of me."

"Why?"

He shrugged. "Who knows? The stuff on the news, probably. The whole story's not there and I know the director's only releasing what he deems relevant, but Penny knows I'm not with Dupree any longer and she knows I haven't gone in for help. I guess it doesn't look good to her."

"It doesn't look good to anyone." She paused. "The team thinks you're a double agent."

His nostrils flared. "A double agent?" He laughed. A short sound that held no humor. "No. No way." He waved the weapon. "See?

That's why I need this. I didn't want it to get ugly between us with me answering all your questions and you having to apologize. This way, we just cut out the harsh part."

"Then prove yourself."

"What do you mean?"

"Let me cuff you and put you in custody," she proposed. "I'll take you in and we'll get all this sorted out back in Billings."

"Take me in? Seriously?" Star shifted beside Harper and Jake's eyes flicked to the animal then back to Harper. "That's what it's going to take? Harper, come on."

For a moment she wavered. Then stiffened her spine. "Yes, that's what it's going to take."

He sighed and dropped his head for a moment, all the while still holding the gun on her. Different thoughts raced through her mind. Visions of diving across the table and taking him down danced with him surrendering. What would he do?

"All right."

"All right, what?"

"Take me in." He set his weapon on the table and held out his hands. "Cuff me."

She hesitated, watching his eyes. But they were shuttered. Hooded. Everything in her warned her not to trust him. "Move the gun farther away."

He rolled his eyes and shoved it off the table. It hit the floor with a thud. "Satisfied?"

"Somewhat."

He held his hands back out to her.

Lips tight, she stood, pulled the cuffs from the case on her belt, and slid them across the table. "Put them on."

He took them and clicked one around his wrist then fumbled with the other. He tried again and almost got it—until he dropped it. He held his arms back out. "Just get this over with, will you?"

Still she hesitated, searching his face, his body language. Unable to get a clear reading on him, her internal alarms screaming at her, she decided she really had no choice. If he went for the weapon that was now on the floor, she'd have time to stop him. Then again, he could have another on him. "Pull your pants legs up from the ankle."

"You think I have another weapon?"

"Just do it."

With a grunt, he leaned over and did as she asked. He looked clean. When he straightened, he held his hands out yet again, the one cuff dangling from his right hand.

"Not yet. Turn around and let me see your back. Pull your shirt up."

He laughed. "Turn my back on you? Are you

kidding? No way. You're cuffing my hands in front of me. Pretty sure I'm not going to be able to reach a weapon at my back."

She stared at him and he sighed. He kept an eye on her over his shoulder, but did as she asked. He lifted the hem of his shirt and clearly had no more weapons on him. He turned full circle and held out his hands.

She stepped forward and reached for the cuff to finish the job.

His arm swung and the cuff caught her in the forehead. Pain shot through her and she cried out, falling to her knees. Her vision went dark for a second.

Jake dove for the gun. Star barked and lunged at Jake. Harper blinked and saw him grab the weapon he'd tossed and turn it on Star. Star latched onto his arm. Jake cried out. "Call her off or I'll shoot her!"

"Star, release!"

Star stopped her attack and released her grip on his arm, but she didn't back away from Jake. She kept herself between him and Harper.

"Sit, Star."

The well-trained animal sat, her gaze bouncing between Harper and Jake.

Jake stumbled away from Star and cursed.

Harper raised a hand to her bleeding forehead. She'd ignored her better judgment and paid for it. "Guess you're not going in peacefully after all, huh? Did that whole story you just spun have any truth at all in it?"

Jake sighed, walked over and grabbed her arm. "Shut up, Harper." Star growled and rose to her feet.

"Star, stay." Harper quickly threw out the command before Jake could turn the gun back on the dog and possibly pull the trigger.

Jake pulled her to her feet then shoved her back into the chair. He reached behind him and grabbed a coil of rope from the counter. "Well, I was going to use this to do a little rappelling, but guess I can use it to keep you out of the way instead. And I've got to get out of here. I'm sure someone's looking for you."

He bound her hands, then bent to tie her feet. She kicked out and caught him in the shoulder. He fell backward with a shouted curse and she lunged from the chair toward the door.

A hard hand wrapped around her left ankle and pulled her back toward the chair. She slid across the floor like a sled on ice. He was big and much stronger than she. "You are one feisty little thing, aren't you?"

He picked her up as though she weighed no more than a bag of sugar and tossed her back into the chair. This time he turned her sideways and tied her hands to the back of the chair.

"Harper!"

Harper froze at the sound of her name coming from outside the cabin. "Harper! Where are you?"

Riley.

Jake pointed the weapon at her. "Call out and you die. And he'll be next."

She snapped her lips closed and fumed. Jake knelt and finished tying her ankles together. "We're going to find you, you know."

"No, you won't. Which is why there's no point in killing you. I'm just trying to slow you down so I can get a head start and disappear."

Riley called out once more, but this time his voice sounded fainter. He was walking away from her and Jake and the cabin.

Which was good. It might just save his life.

Her head throbbed where the cuffs had cut the skin and warm blood trickled down her cheek. "They'll be here soon, Jake. They're looking for me even now and you know it."

"I know."

"So everything you just told me was a lie."

"Not everything, just most of it." He shrugged. "I was trying to get of here peacefully, but you weren't going to cooperate."

"You're just going to leave me here?"

He leaned in and lifted a finger to stroke her cheek. She bit back the gag reflex and glared at him. "I'm not like the Duprees," he said softly. "I don't just kill to kill."

"You just kill if you think you're going to be caught and brought in."

He narrowed his eyes and Harper wondered if she'd gone too far. Then he shrugged. "But, I *have* been...*corrupted*, I guess you could say. I've had a taste of true power. I've held millions of dollars in my hands." His eyes took on a strange glow that Harper realized was greed. The sight made her want to cringe. But she refused. "Do you know what that feels like?" he asked.

"No."

He smiled and it was almost sad. "No, you wouldn't. Because once you've felt it, there's no going back." His gaze dropped to her lips. "I could kiss you now, you know. I've always wanted to."

Her heart stuttered and she strained away from him. "You could force it, but I don't want it now any more than I wanted it when we worked together."

His nostrils flared then he smiled and started to lower his head. "Let's see if you feel the same way after."

A noise at the door jerked his attention from

her and he swung the weapon around. Harper stiffened, her heart racing. Who could it be?

Morrow raced from the shelter.

FOURTEEN

Riley's side hurt. He'd worn the vest but the bullet had found an unprotected area just below it. He was sure that had been on purpose. Maybe Van was a better marksman than he'd given him credit for. He ignored the burn along with all of his other aches and pains.

Because none of that mattered. He had to find Harper. He'd called her name, but gotten no response. Perhaps she was in trouble, either having met up with Morrow or Blackman. Then again, maybe…

Maybe nothing.

She was in trouble. His gut shouted it.

Max and the others were headed in his direction. He hoped. But he wasn't even sure where he was and could only give them directions based on the location of the sun.

He'd managed to follow Harper's and Star's tracks until he got deep into the wooded area. At that point, he lost them. He had some tracking skills, but they weren't good enough to figure out which way she and the dog had gone once they'd veered off the path.

He did think there was a third person with them, which made him leery and alert.

"Harper? Can you hear me?"

"She's still not answering," Max said, stating the obvious. "We need to find her ASAP."

More of the obvious.

Riley sent up prayers for her safety and his own. Returning to Asher was paramount. He couldn't get killed and break his promise to be there for his nephew. "Priorities," he muttered.

"What was that?" Max asked.

"Nothing. Just reminding myself I can't die."

"Right. Remember that."

Riley came to another clearing along the river and noticed the small cabin set back up on a hill. He started toward it, glancing over his shoulder, hating that he was so exposed.

But if there was anyone in that cabin, they might have seen or heard something that could help lead him to Van or Harper. Right now, he preferred Harper. He was almost desperate to know she was safe.

As he approached the cabin, he looked down and thought he saw paw prints. Star?

"Harper? Harper!"

A footstep behind him.

He spun to see Van Blackman taking aim. Riley dove behind the nearest tree.

Harper's ears tuned in to the sounds around her even while her head throbbed. Had Riley called her name? "Riley?"

She struggled with the ropes and froze when she heard a sound in the door. Had Jake come back?

A shuffling, snuffling sound reached her. "Jake? Riley?"

A shadow fell across the entryway and a furry head rounded the corner.

Harper sucked in a breath at the sight of the wolf. The animal spotted her and bared its teeth while a low growl rumbled in its chest.

Star went into a barking frenzy and lunged. The wolf bolted and Harper's shoulders slumped. Star returned to her side and nudged her. "I know, girl. We've got to get out of here."

She finally managed to get her hands free of the back of the chair. That piece of the rope dropped to the dirt floor. And while her hands were still tied together, at least she could move. She managed to get hold of the earpiece still dangling over her shoulder and slip it into her ear. She could hear the conversation even though she wouldn't be able to call out until she got her radio in hand. Right now, the team was silent.

Where was Riley?

"You see him?"

Max's voice came to her.

"Negative," Ian said.

"Keep looking. He's shot so he might be passed out somewhere."

Who was shot? *Riley?* Had she heard that right?

She tugged her feet up closer and with her bound hands pulled her pants leg up to expose the knife she kept on, strapped to the inside of her right ankle. It was a good thing Jake had grabbed her left one and not the right one or he would have felt it.

She snagged it and worked it under the ropes holding her ankles together. The sharp blade sliced through the fiber.

Now the tricky part.

Harper sat in the chair and pulled her feet up to rest on the seat. She clasped the handle of the knife between her knees and turned the blade outward. She brought her hands up and slid the rope up and down against the razor-sharp edge until her wrists fell free.

She shoved the knife back into the case then stood. Dizziness hit her and she swayed for a moment while she got her balance. Finally, she thought she could move without falling and stumbled to the counter to grab her radio.

"Max. Ian?"

"Harper! Where are you?"

"I'm not exactly sure, but Jake overpowered me and tied me up in a little cabin where he's been staying. It's near the river and that's about all I know. I'm going to retrace my steps. Where's Riley?"

"Haven't heard from him in a while," Max said. "He let us know he'd been shot and then we lost contact with him."

Shot? "How bad?"

"Not bad. Just a graze."

Another wave of dizziness hit her and she shut her eyes while she waited for it to pass. "All right, I'll start looking."

"Are you hurt?"

"Not as bad as I could have been. Jake got me in the head with my cuffs. If you come across him, don't fall for anything he says. He's definitely a double agent."

"10-4 on that."

His disappointment came through loud and clear. Harper rearmed herself with the weapon Jake had tossed onto the counter then called Star to her side and stepped out of the cabin.

"Riley!" She knew he'd called her name. So where was he?

She sprinted around the side of the little house and stopped when she saw Van Blackman aiming a gun at Riley. She lifted hers. "Federal agent! Put the weapon down, Blackman, or you die."

The man spun and aimed the weapon at her. She started to squeeze the trigger when Riley leaped out from behind the tree and tackled the man.

Riley threw a solid punch and caught Van in the mouth. Van's head snapped back even as the man rolled and snagged his weapon. As Riley went in for another hit, Van brought the weapon up against the side of Riley's head.

From the corner of his eye, Riley saw Harper, her own weapon trained on Van, and knew the only reason she hadn't shot was because she was afraid of hitting him.

And now Van had him hostage, his harsh breaths echoing in his ear while the barrel of the gun dug into his temple.

"You're a hard man to kill, Martelli," Blackman snarled, pulling Riley to his feet while keeping the gun steady.

Riley stood and swayed. He was running out of strength and gritted his teeth to keep his knees locked. "You're a hard man to find,

Blackman," he managed to say, his voice sounding a lot more firm than he'd thought it would.

Blackman laughed. "Well, I guess the hunt is over."

"I guess it is." Weakness and nausea swept over Riley and his side flamed with pain from the bullet wound. Truthfully, it was all he could do to remain standing. But falling or passing out weren't options. "Are you going to come peacefully or am I going to have to shoot you? I know which one I'm hoping for."

Van laughed. "I think you're delusional. I'm the one with the weapon on you. And if your pretty girlfriend doesn't drop hers, you die."

He let his gaze lock on hers. "Don't drop it."

Rage seethed in the look she shot the man behind him. "Van, I can't drop my gun. You're done. You can't win this."

"Of course I can. It's simple. If I'm going to prison, Riley dies. If you let me go, he lives. Are you willing to sacrifice his life for mine?"

"Don't listen to him. He'll just come back and finish the job later," Riley ground out. "If you drop your weapon, he'll simply shoot both of us." The gun pressed tighter against his head and Riley winced. "Here. What about this? I'll go with you. You can drop me off somewhere and it'll all be done. You'll be free and Harper and I'll be alive. She has nothing to do with this, Van. This is between you and me."

"Not anymore. You brought her here. You brought them all here. You and the local police, I can outrun and outsmart." He shook his head. "The FBI is a different story."

Van seemed to be favoring his left arm. "What's wrong with your arm?"

"Nothing's wrong with my arm."

"I shot him, that's what's wrong with it," Harper said. "So you left a note on my door telling me to stay away because you were mad Riley brought in the FBI?" she said as she moved sideways. "Did you really think that was going to work?"

Van laughed and turned with Riley in front of him. "It was worth a shot."

"So what are you going to do?" Harper asked. "If you shoot him, you'll just have the FBI on your tail even harder than we already are."

"I never planned to kill you in the beginning, Riley. What happened to Charlotte was tragic and I deeply regret it. But I'm not going to jail. You're like a dog with a bone. You just don't give up." He paused and a look of regret crossed his face. "I didn't mean to shoot Asher."

Riley's jaw tightened. With effort, he restrained himself from trying to spin out of the man's grasp so he could tear him apart with his bare hands. "But you did."

"Is he okay?"

"That's none of your business."

"Is he going to be ok—" He broke off with a shout and the weapon slipped from Riley's temple.

"Bite!" Harper yelled the command. Riley let his legs give way and slumped to the ground even as he caught a blur of motion from the corner of his eye.

Van let out another harsh scream and fell to the ground, Star's powerful jaws locked around his forearm.

Riley rolled. Pain held him frozen. Blackness swirled and he had a hard time keeping his eyes open. The moment passed and he was finally able to catch his breath and roll to his side, his gun pressing into his hip.

Van lay on his stomach, silent and still. Harper called Star off and the animal backed up, her focus never wavering from the man on the ground. She had her radio button depressed while she kept her weapon on Van.

"Are you okay, Riley?" she asked.

"What's happening? What's going on? Someone report in now!"

Max's voice came through the headset, but Riley couldn't answer.

"Suspect down," Harper stated. "Approaching him."

Riley took another breath and his vision cleared.

Harper stepped up to Van and he lashed out with a foot, knocking her in the knee. Harper went down once again, dropping her gun. She scrambled to get out of his reach, but Van was too quick, landing a punch in her stomach. The air whooshed from her and she bent, now on all fours.

"Harper!"

Move! Riley's brain issued the order, but his body was slow to respond.

Van grabbed the knife from her now-exposed ankle case and raised it over Harper's head. "You should have listened to my warning."

Riley's fingers fumbled for the weapon beneath him, then grasped it.

He raised it and fired. Then fired again.

Van's eyes widened.

The knife slipped from his suddenly slack grip and he fell to the ground with a thud.

Harper let out a gasp and Riley crawled over to her. She gasped again and made a wheezing sound. "Breathe," Riley said softly, "just breathe."

She nodded and took a few more seconds to get her breath. Then she pushed him away and reached out to lay two fingers on Van's neck. Her eyes lifted to his. "He's dead," she whispered then fell back to the ground with a grunt. "I'll get up…in…a minute."

She lay there for a full minute and a half then rolled into a sitting position.

"I should be glad." He looked at the man who'd been in his nightmares for the past two months. The man who'd killed his sister and altered the lives of his family forever.

"You're not?"

He shook his head. "I don't know what I am, to be honest. Except glad it's over." He sighed heavily. "And sad it came to this." He frowned and touched her forehead gently. "Are you okay? He got you with a hard hit."

"That was from the cuffs earlier. I'm fine."

"Cuffs?"

She wave a hand in dismissal. "You saved my life."

He shrugged. "I figure I owed you."

She smiled and he looked back at Van and shuddered. He hauled himself to his feet and held out a hand to help her up.

Star watched them, her gaze bouncing from one to the other. Then her ears perked and she turned.

Riley saw Max, Ian and the other dogs heading their way. "Well, better late than never, right?"

Harper grimaced. "Right."

Riley stepped back, nursing his wounds, doing his best to ignore the pain pounding through him while he watched the others gather around Harper and demand to know what had happened.

While she explained, he realized he'd fallen in love with her. In spite of his determined efforts to prevent it from happening, his heart had gone and betrayed him. Her strength had impressed him, her beauty ensnared him. Limitless courage, heart rending compassion, a selfless love for those she put first in her life… all of those traits belonged to Harper, and his heart had fallen. Hard. It had let her in in spite of his resistance.

But he couldn't love her. Loving someone else just wasn't going to happen. Because love hurt.

He'd loved his mother and Asher and he'd be there for them, but that was it. Once he'd made the decision, the pain in his heart actually rivaled the one in his side and the rest of his battered body.

And then he had no more time to think. The team now surrounded him, questioned him and demanded to know that he was all right.

"I'm fine, really."

"Well, you're going to the hospital."

"I don't need a hospital." He touched his side. "It's just a flesh wound."

"You're going. Period," Max said in a stern tone.

Riley sighed. "Fine, but I'm going to the same hospital where my nephew is."

"Deal." Max nodded to Ian. "Let's get some vehicles up here so we can take care of this mess." He looked down at Van. "And a coroner." His eyes took in the cabin. "Is there a blanket in there?"

Harper nodded. "I'll get it."

"You stay put." Max stepped into the cabin. He was gone so long Harper almost went after him. But he finally reappeared carrying the blanket from the cot.

"That's part of a crime scene, you know," Harper said.

"Yeah. That's why I processed that area before I took the blanket."

They fell silent and simply waited. Harper finally heard the sound of engines heading their way. She glanced at Riley and wondered what was going on with him. He was so closed off and shuttered. She slipped over to him. "You okay?"

"Not really."

"What's wrong?" she asked quietly.

He shook his head. "I just need some time to think."

"About?"

"Everything."

"Want to talk about it?"

"No."

She raised a brow. "All right." She wasn't going to pry it out of him. If he wanted to talk, he knew where to find her.

He raked a bandaged hand through the hair that already stood on end. He opened his mouth to speak then shut it when Leo pulled up.

With an ambulance right behind him.

Leo climbed from the Suburban. "Any sign of Jake?" Harper asked.

"No, afraid not."

She pursed her lips and nodded. Two paramedics approached and she was surprised Riley didn't argue about being checked out.

When they approached her, she sighed and figured she might as well be a good sport as well.

Three hours later, she sat on a gurney in the emergency department, absently checking her email on her phone and waiting to be released. She had the all-clear healthwise, with simple orders to rest and heal. She had no concussion from the hit with the cuffs, just a cut and a bad knot. It would heal.

She sighed and dialed Dylan's number.

"Hello?"

"Dylan, you sound a little tense."

"Oh. It's you."

A laugh slipped from her. "Sorry to disappoint you."

"No, no. It's okay. I'm sorry. What's up?"

"I just called to say thanks for all your hard work on the fund-raiser for Asher. He's doing really well."

"Aw, you're welcome," he replied. "That was a fun project to do. At least I knew it would have a good outcome."

"So what else is going on? What's gotten you so stressed?"

"It's still Zara. I haven't heard from her in almost a week. I know she's working hard at Quantico with her training and everything, but she's my fiancée. I need to hear from her."

Harper frowned. "That *is* disturbing." It just occurred to her that Zara hadn't answered the text she'd sent her a few days ago.

"Thank you! See? It's driving me *nuts*. I've called and called and gotten nothing. I'm ready to fly out there and start knocking down doors until someone gives me some answers."

"Let me call Quantico and see what I can find out."

He exhaled an audible sigh of relief. "I would be forever grateful."

"All right, give me a little time. I'll be in touch soon."

She hung up and dialed the number that would take her past all the security and right to the person she needed. When the call center picked up, she said, "This is Harper Prentiss. I'd like to talk to Zara Fielding. She hasn't been in touch with her fiancé for the past week and we're all a little concerned."

"All trainees are indisposed at the moment, but more information will be forthcoming."

"*Indisposed?* What does that mean?"

"I'm sorry, I can't offer anything more than that."

"That's a canned response and you know it. What's going on?"

"As I said, more information will be forthcoming."

Harper sighed. She wasn't going to get anything else out of the woman. "All right, thanks."

"Have a nice day."

"Right. You, too." She hung up and frowned. Something was definitely wrong. She called Dylan back and he answered on the first ring.

"What did you find out?"

She told him her conversation with the attendant.

"I don't like it," he said.

"Okay, here's what I think. I think Zara and her team are probably in some type of safe house or something like that. I really don't think you need to worry. Remember, the best of the best is looking out for her and the other trainees."

"Yeah, but sometimes things can go wrong even for the best of the best."

She had to agree. "Hang in there, Dylan. We'll figure it out."

He blew out a breath. "Thanks for trying, Harper."

"Sure thing."

She disconnected just as a knock on her door brought her head up. "Come in."

Riley stepped inside and shut the door behind him. "Hey."

Still a little miffed at his aloof treatment from earlier, Harper debated about answering him then decided not to be childish. "Hey."

He gestured to the chair next to the bed. "You mind?"

"It's all yours."

He seated himself and closed his eyes for a moment.

"It's been a long day."

"Yes."

"I just came from Asher's room."

She softened. She simply couldn't stay mad at him. "How's he doing?"

"Great." His throat worked and she wondered what he was trying to say. "He can feel his feet and wiggle his toes."

Tears filled her eyes. She couldn't help it. She'd come to love Asher in a very short period time. "That's wonderful, Riley."

"Yes. It is."

"How is your head? Do you have a concussion?"

"A slight one, but the scans were clear." He touched his side. "The gunshot wound has been cleaned and stitched up and my hands have new bandages."

"Sounds like you're good to go."

"I am." He paused and ran a hand over his chin. "So what now? Morrow's still out there."

"Which means we're still looking for him."

He nodded. "It just hit me while I was watching Asher that you and your team are really good people. The real deal."

She gave a low laugh. "You just now realized that?"

He shook his head. "This isn't coming out right."

"I'm sorry. Go ahead."

"I think after Charlotte died, I lost what little faith I had in humanity. I closed myself off to all but my mother and Asher."

"Understandable," she murmured.

"Maybe. But wrong, too. Asher wouldn't have had that surgery yet without you and your team. I'll never be able to repay you."

"We'd never ask."

He smiled. "I know. You all have restored my faith that not everyone is just looking out for themselves. Some people actually care about others and look out for them, help them. I needed to see that and guess God knew that."

"He does give us what we need when we need it."

"Even when we don't realize we need it sometimes."

She laughed. "Sometimes it works that way, doesn't it?"

"I..."

"What?"

He cleared his throat then said in a low, rough voice, "I don't want this to be the end."

"Of what?"

"Us."

Her heart sped up. "There's an us?"

"I sure hope so." He settled on the edge of her bed and leaned in, his eyes intense.

Harper swallowed and tried to still her suddenly rapid pulse.

"How do you feel about long-distance relationships?" he asked, taking her hands in his.

"I don't know. I've never had one."

"Well, I don't like them."

She blinked. "Oh. Okay."

"When Asher can travel, I want to bring him and Mom out to Billings and see you."

"Really?" she whispered.

"Really. And then we'll have that dinner date we still haven't had."

"I'll be waiting."

He leaned over and kissed her. Time stopped for that brief moment. She kissed him back and realized how very much she wanted it to work between them. When he pulled back, his eyes were warm, glowing almost. She wondered if hers looked the same.

He smiled. "See you soon."

FIFTEEN

Three weeks later
Billings, Montana
K-9 Headquarters

Riley pressed the phone to his ear. He'd made the call to Max after much pacing and soul-searching. Asher watched him from the sofa across the room. "What do you think? Will you help me?"

"I think it's a great idea," Max said.

"So you think she'll go for it?"

"I guess all you can do is give it your best shot, but yes, I think she will. Did she tell you that she found her father?"

"Yes." He paused. "She went to see him at the prison, didn't she?"

Max sighed. "Yeah, and she wouldn't let anyone go with her. She said this was something she had to do on her own."

"That's what she told me." He'd offered to

go with her and she'd turned him down flat. He understood. Sort of. But still didn't like it. "All right, keep this all under your hat and I'll see you soon."

Riley hung up with Max and went back to pacing. Asher giggled. "What's so funny, Champ?"

"You."

"What do you mean?" He swiped a hand across his forehead then rubbed it on his jeans.

"Why are you all sweaty?"

Riley paused, wiped his forehead again then shot him a wry smile. "I guess it's called nerves, kid."

Asher blinked at him. "Huh?"

He sighed. "Can you keep a secret?"

His nephew's eyes went wide. "A secret? Like a real live never-ever-tell secret?"

"Well, we're going to tell it eventually, but yeah."

Asher frowned and puckered his lips. After about a six-second delay, he nodded. "I've thought about it. I can keep a secret."

"Great. So here's what we're going to do…"

Harper sat at the conference table wondering why Max had called her in. Then Ian Slade stepped inside and her confusion mounted. "What's this all about? Do you know?"

"Not a clue. I was hoping you knew something."

She shrugged. "Guess we'll find out soon enough. How are you doing?"

He shrugged. "I want Jake Morrow in custody."

"I know."

"How are you feeling?" he asked.

"Like new. All healed up. No more headaches."

"And Riley?"

Just thinking of him brought a smile to her face. "He's perfect."

Ian laughed. "He's a man. Trust me, he's not perfect."

She lightly punched his shoulder. "He's perfect for me. We've FaceTimed every day since I've been back here. And Asher is making remarkable progress. He's walking on his own and even running a little."

Ian's expression softened. "That's wonderful."

The door opened and Max stepped inside. "Thanks for coming in, guys."

"We had a choice?" Ian smirked.

"You're a funny guy, Ian."

Ian sobered. "Okay, boss, what's this all about?"

Max looked Ian in the eye and Harper

frowned. "I know about your connection to the Duprees."

Ian stiffened and his face went blank. "It's not a secret."

"But you've treated it like one."

"What's going on?" Harper asked.

Max continued to hold Ian's gaze. "I haven't told anyone else, but I wanted Harper to be in on this discussion. She needs to know."

"Know what?"

Ian sighed and nodded. "All right." He met Harper's gaze. "The Duprees killed my parents."

Harper gasped. "What?"

"It's a long story, but it happened when I was sixteen years old. I vowed to bring them down one day."

Max turned his attention to her. "I wouldn't have said anything except we're getting close and I want Ian to have backup and eyes on him at all times. If something happens, I don't want the Duprees to be able to claim Ian acted unprofessionally."

"Boss—"

"I don't think you would. I'm saying I want to be able to back up anything that goes down with an eyewitness. You understand? This isn't about revenge. It's about justice."

Ian nodded and stood. "Sometimes the two

are one and the same." He walked to the window and stared out.

Max frowned and Harper could tell he was worried about Ian.

"Are we done here?" Ian asked.

"We're done."

Ian left and Max sighed.

Harper crossed her arms and leaned back in her chair. "Ian's one of the best, Max. He'll be all right."

Max nodded. "I know he is. I just pray that his personal vow to bring in Angus Dupree to join his nephew in prison doesn't get Ian—or anyone else—killed."

She nodded. "I'll keep an eye on him." She turned to leave.

"Hold on a second, will you?"

Harper raised a brow. "Is there something else?"

"No. I mean yes."

Harper frowned then gave a little laugh. "Okay. Which one is it?"

A knock on the door interrupted them. Max's immediate relief had her extremely curious. Harper stood to answer the door since it was closer to her side of the table, but Max beat her to it.

"Harper!"

The little voice wrangled a gasp from her. "Asher? Riley? What are you guys doing here?"

The little boy stepped carefully, placing one foot in front of the other to finally reach her. He grinned up at her and she gently swung him up into her arms with an exaggerated grunt. "You've gained weight since I last saw you."

"Uncle Riley's been feeding me steak."

"Good for him."

Riley and Max shook hands. Then Riley hugged her and planted a quick hello kiss on her lips. She wanted more, but was as aware of their audience as he was.

"I came to take you to lunch," Riley said. "Can you get away?"

Harper looked at Max and he nodded. "Go. Enjoy."

"Thanks, Max."

Asher refused to let go of her hand after she set him on his feet so she held it and Riley took the other one. Asher walked between them with a smile on his face.

Once out of the building and on the sidewalk, Harper leaned over Asher's head and kissed Riley on the cheek. "How'd you get in and upstairs?"

"I have friends in high places now, remember? Like your coworkers?"

She laughed. "I guess so." She pulled Asher

to her in a quick hug, careful not to knock him off balance. "I can't believe you guys are here. I've missed you."

"I missed you, too," Asher said. "But I'm hungry. Can we eat?"

Riley laughed. "Of course. And we're almost there."

"Where?"

"Three more steps and turn right."

Asher counted his steps out loud then made a sharp right nearly causing Riley to stumble. He caught the boy and helped him open the door to a small café that was one of Harper's favorites.

Petrov's Bakery. "Oh, yum. We get pastries here for our meetings. I think if they quit supplying them, we'd quit meeting."

Riley waved a hand to the man behind the counter and he nodded with a smile. "I rented out the back room so we could have it to ourselves."

"What? Oh, how fun."

SIXTEEN

Riley led the way to the back. He'd arranged this all with Max and Max had led him to the café. The table had been set for three and he pulled out the chair for her. She settled into it. At one of the other places, a small bell was next to the water glass. Riley smiled. Perfect.

"Wow," Harper said, "thanks, guys. This is so lovely."

Nerves attacked him and he drew in a deep breath. "I'm glad you like it. Asher and I put a lot of thought into it, didn't we?"

"We sure did. Are you going to show her the—"

He clamped a hand over the child's mouth. "Not yet."

Asher's eyes went wide. Then he giggled. "Okay." He looked at Harper. "It's a secret."

"A secret, huh?" She slid a glance at Riley and he put on his most innocent smile.

She narrowed her eyes and he cleared his

throat. The waiter arrived and spared him for a moment. After placing their order, he took a sip of his water then set the glass aside. "Any word on Morrow?"

She shook her head. "No. But we're not giving up. We'll find him."

Harper put the napkin in her lap. "Thank you, this is wonderful."

Asher laughed. "You already said that. Well, actually, I guess you said lovely, but it's the same thing, right?"

Harper grinned. "Yes, I suppose so. But it's true."

Riley smiled as well. "How did your visit with your father go today?"

The joy left her face and Riley could have kicked himself for bringing up the subject. He blamed his nerves for doing so.

Harper sighed. "It went well, I think. I was rather surprised at his reception. He said he'd thought of me often and wondered what I ended up like. You should have seen his face when I told him what I did for a living, though. Now that was quite a sight to see."

"And he didn't get up and walk out?"

"No." She gave an odd smile and he thought she looked amused. "He seemed…proud."

"You expected him to have a different reaction."

"Absolutely. He's spent his life hating cops and their authority and then he winds up with a daughter for one. It was sort of funny. In a weird kind of way."

"So, do you think you'll go see him again?"

Harper nodded. "Yes. I'm working on forgiving him. I asked him if he'd be willing to be transferred here to Billings and he said he would. I told him I'd see if I could arrange it." She drew in a breath. "I think the more I see him, the easier that will be. Maybe."

Riley lifted a brow. "You really think you'll forgive him?"

Harper smiled. "I think it will be a daily journey. But I think, with God's help, it's one that I have to take."

Riley reached over and wrapped a hand around her warm fingers. "I understand," he said. "And it's a journey you don't have to take alone."

Harper blinked back tears. "You can't know how much that means to me."

Riley grinned. "I might have a pretty good idea."

"Uncle Riley, aren't you going to show her—"

Riley clapped his free hand over Asher's mouth again. "Not yet."

Harper giggled. He didn't think he'd ever

heard that sound come from her before. "I think you'd better show me whatever it is you haven't shown me yet."

Riley sighed. If he kept dragging it out, Asher was going to spill the beans. "Well, Asher, Mom and I have decided to move to Billings, Montana."

Harper froze and her eyes went wide. "What?"

He shrugged. "We miss you. And my job is portable. So to speak." She still looked stunned and Riley's palms started to sweat. "Um, is that okay?"

A huge smile spread across her face. "It's more than okay. It's wonderful!"

Riley's heart pounded. "Oh good. We were hoping for that reaction."

"Of course. I couldn't be happier."

Tears stood in her eyes, bolstering his courage for the next part of the conversation. "So, Harper..."

She swiped a stray tear. "Yes?"

"I want to be that man."

She blinked. "What?"

"You remember our conversation where you told me to get over myself?"

She flushed. "I remember."

"You were right. And as soon as I said I didn't want to be that man, I regretted the words. I love you, Harper. We've been through a lot and come out on the other side and it took almost losing you to realize I don't want to live life without you." He glanced at Asher. "Make that *we* don't want to live without you. Right, Champ?"

"Uh-huh. That's right."

The stunned look returned. Then she swallowed. "I didn't think I'd hear those words quite this soon."

He frowned. "Too soon?"

"No. Not at all. I've imagined you saying them almost every day and now...you have."

"Yes. I have."

She swallowed. "I love you, too, Riley. I think I realized it when you held that little puppy all the way to the rescue farm."

He went speechless for a moment. "I...wow."

"Is it time yet?" Asher whispered.

Riley laughed and handed the child the bell. "Go for it."

Gleefully, Asher took the bell and skipped to the door.

Harper blinked. She'd forgotten the bell was there. Asher stood at the entrance into the main part of the restaurant and rang the bell three times. Then he ran back to the table and sat, folding his hands in his lap. Harper swung her gaze back to Riley. "What in the world are you two up to?"

"Mr. Petrov is bringing the—"

Riley clapped his hand back over Asher's mouth. The little guy's eyes crinkled at the corners and Harper laughed. Riley had better hurry up with his surprise or Asher was going to let her in on it.

"Are we ready, Mr. Martelli?"

Mr. Petrov walked into the room carrying a bag.

That moved?

The robust man handed it to Riley who quickly set it on the floor. "Thank you."

"Yes sir, I have your food for you when you're ready."

"Just a few more minutes."

"Of course. Take as long as you like." He bustled from the room and Harper blinked as a little yap came from under the table.

Amused, she grinned. "Did that bag just bark?"

Riley sighed and rolled his eyes. "Yes, but just hold on a minute."

"But Uncle Riley—"

"Ash—"

But Asher had already clamped his own hand over his own mouth. Harper lost it. She laughed. A deep belly laugh that rolled all the way up and out of her mouth. Tears leaked from her eyes and it was a good minute before she could control her mirth. Riley handed her a napkin and she dabbed at the wetness trying not to completely destroy the little makeup she had on. "Oh, my, Asher. You're just too much."

Riley, too, was laughing and shaking his head. He reached down and she heard the bag rustle. Then a little black and brown head with floppy ears popped up. Harper gasped. "The puppy."

"Yes."

"You went back and got him."

"I did."

"He's grown a bit."

"That's because he eats more than a fifteen-year-old boy does. Here." He handed the squirming pup over to her. She held the puppy under her chin and he nipped it. He sported a red ribbon and smelled like all little puppies smell. Love and innocence and laughter. She scratched a silky ear and laughed again, marveling that her heart could feel so full.

Something hard bounced against her hand and she looked down. Another gasp slipped from her lips. Her insides turned to mush and her muscles went weak. She met Riley's gaze. And read so many emotions there. Emotions she was sure were mirrored in her own eyes.

She lifted the ring that he'd tied into the ribbon and stared at the beautiful diamond.

He lifted a brow. "Do you like it?"

"Of course she likes it," Asher blurted. "Who doesn't like puppies?"

Riley stroked his nephew's head fondly, but his eyes never left hers. With shaking fingers, Harper tucked the little body under her arm and released the ribbon around the puppy's neck.

The diamond slid off the end of the cloth and fell into her palm. "It's beautiful."

"Will you marry me?"

"Us," Asher said. "'Cuz I live with Uncle Riley now. Mimi does too."

"Yes," Riley said, "sorry, us. We're a package deal, I'm afraid."

Tears spilled over her dark lashes. She tried to speak, but realized nothing was coming out. She settled for nodding.

"Yay!" Asher jumped up and pumped a fist in the air. "She said yes, Uncle Riley, she said yes!"

Harper gave another watery laugh. Riley stood and walked around the table to take the puppy from her arms. "Here, Champ, hold Rudolph for a minute."

Harper raised a brow. "Rudolph?"

"Don't ask me why. A six-year-old named him."

"Oh, right."

He held his hand out. "Could I hold the ring?"

"Are you going to give it back?"

He chuckled. "Yes."

"Okay, then." She dropped it into his hand. With his other hand, he raised her to her feet then went down on one knee and looked up at her. "Are you sure?"

"More sure than anything in the world."

He slipped the ring on her finger then stood.

"You gotta kiss her now," Asher stage-whispered.

"Thanks, Champ, I guess I do."

He leaned over and placed his warm lips on hers. Harper's knees wanted to melt so she locked her arms around his neck and kissed him right back with all the love and emotion she had in her heart.

"That's good enough," Asher said impatiently. "I'm hungry."

Harper opened her eyes and looked into Riley's. "I love you. Later?"

"Absolutely."

Asher handed the puppy back to Riley, grabbed the bell and ran to the door to ring it again.

Mr. Petrov entered right away followed by two of his workers carrying their food. The restaurant owner took the puppy. "Enjoy this star of a new life, my friends. I pray many blessings over you and your family."

Harper sucked in a breath. Yes. Family. Prayers and blessings.

God was good.

Prayers were answered and dreams came true.

She knew that for a fact and couldn't wait to see what the future held.

She grinned at her guys and sent up a silent prayer of thanks to the One who'd made it all work out.

Riley's hand reached across the table and gripped hers and she reached for Asher's hand. He took it then gripped his uncle's.

Harper looked at their hands. Gripped tight in a circle.

A never-ending circle of love.

* * * * *

If you enjoyed BOUNTY HUNTER, the next book in the CLASSIFIED K-9 UNIT *series is BODYGUARD by Shirlee McCoy. And don't miss a book in the series:*

GUARDIAN by Terri Reed
SHERIFF by Laura Scott
SPECIAL AGENT by Valerie Hansen
BOUNTY HUNTER by Lynette Eason
BODYGUARD by Shirlee McCoy
TRACKER by Lenora Worth
CLASSIFIED K-9 UNIT CHRISTMAS by Terri Reed and Lenora Worth

Dear Reader,

Thank you so much for joining me on Riley and Harper's journey to catch the bad guys and find true love. Riley had a hard time with his sister's murder (who wouldn't?) and Harper had grown up in a tough situation. But she'd made peace with it and now trusted God to lead her. Riley was mad at God about the whole situation, but gradually sees that while on this earth, people with free will are going to make bad choices that affect other people's lives in ways that irrevocably change them…and not always for the better. He decided he didn't want Van to "win" and was able to move past the bitterness and anger in order to find peace and joy and a new life with Harper and Asher. I pray if there's bitterness and anger in your life, you can find the same joy and peace, a life filled with God's blessings and goodness. I hope you'll look for the other books in this series. They're all written by different, talented authors! Books 5 and 6 release after this one so be sure to tune in to find out what happens to Jake and Penny Potter! I love to hear from readers. Find me on Facebook at *www.facebook.com/lynette.eason* or Twitter at @lynetteeason. My website is *www.lynetteeason.com*, where you can learn more about me and my books!

Blessings to you,

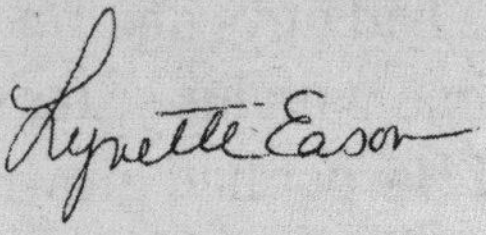